STONE

Duncan Fatz

This edition published 2011 by
Lulu Press, Inc. a subsidiary of
Lulu Enterprises, Inc. 3101
Hillsborough Street, Raleigh, NC
27607, United States

ISBN 978 1 4478 3212 6

Cover design by Duncan Fatz

Book design by Duncan Fatz

ACKNOWLEDGEMENTS

This book is a work of fiction but based on real events and anecdotes.

I would like to thank J &S for supplying the idea which set this work in motion, my mother for supplying further anecdotes, S for helping me with the research, and my wonderful family, N, D, M & J for inspiring me to release it, while not forgetting my dear brother who has always said, 'Go for it!'

This work commenced in the early 1990s and, although it could be updated and perhaps improved for today's society, it acts as a time capsule that serves its purpose best by being set in stone.

Contents

STONE

Sparkle In The Rain

Sweeping over the humpbacked bridge as smoothly as a rising trout, the Porsche sped along the country road; the throb of its engine reverberating between the dry stone walls. A moment later and the engine's roar was replaced by a screech which tore violently through the air as, wide wheels clamped in position, the car fought for purchase on the wet glistening tarmac.

The gleaming black symbol of prestige reversed.

As the Cornish sky poured down its venomous rain on the sodden earth, the driver sat within the warm interior of his car, immune to the rain's discomforting properties but not to its dramatic effect. He sat and gazed across the field towards the monolith that towered above the swaying and battered grass. Apparently impervious to the pounding of the rain, it was obvious that the stone had been standing in that same position for a very long time: not only had it stood the test of time, it had passed it with flying colours.

The driver reached for the grey trilby behind his seat and, setting it firmly on his head, stepped into the night. Slowly walking to the large, tumbled, gap in the wall, he stared across the intervening distance towards the stone, and watched in fascination as the rain shimmered on its coal black surface and collected in small pools of trapped moonlight amongst its gnarled features. He tilted his head, to locate the silver orb, fighting for air space with the black clouds, and a trickle of water, freed from the dam of his hat brim, escaped to slither down the back of his neck. He retreated and lowered himself back into the car. He would be back.

Talking Terms

A flash of steel-grey and the swallow rose streaming over the dry stone wall in a rush of air and feathers. The pulse of life beat fiercely within its fragile breast, forcing the tiny bird crashing through time and space at breakneck speed; soon to leave it fused and burnt out at the end of its existence. But, for now, the swallow careered onwards, scything across the tops of the grass stems and stretching up into the clear blue chill of the morning air, so different from the hot muggy skies of South Africa, recently departed, and now, once more, consigned to the map of its race memory.

Twisting in its flight the swallow reacquainted itself with the aerial panorama of the Cornish landscape strewn below: the hill that caught the air and flung it upwards along its many textured sides—providing both lift and lunch for the birds, which could prey on the weaker insects trapped in the grasp of the updraft. The river, cold and full with rain, springing down into the valley and crashing along its restraining banks; its visage dark with the mud and stones that it teased from the ground to carry along its sinuous course. Like an infant clinging to its mother, the river lay partly coiled around the base of the hill, which had given it its birth, growing older and broader in its passage until, with the sharpness of youth grown bold, it struck away from its origins to dive under the red bricked humpbacked bridge which carried the grey road, the mimic in size and shape of the river's flowing passage to the sea.

Tumbling riotously beside its travelling companion the river raced along the road's length, mocking its frozen stasis as they journeyed to their ends. In deadlock the two travelled, until, with an abrupt convulsion, the foaming waters of the river reached another turning point in their career. Swiftly, certainly, sweepingly, the waters surged away from the road and spewed along their broiling passage to tumble through the portal flanked by the two huge stone posts.

The stones, the sentinels. Massive and grey and solid, as old as the hills that had given the streams their birth; they marked the river's course and mirrored its dark uncompromising power. It was the stones, and what lay hidden behind them in the grass, that acted as a beacon for the swallow's navigation.

A black metallic sparkle triggered a response in the swallow and, wheeling around in its flight, the aerial acrobat spotted what it had been searching for—food. The early spring sun had been too weak to coax the yet cold field insects into taking to the wing, but the pungent, still steaming, dung trail into the milking parlour, had baited the fat slow Blue Bottles into flight, and it was on these that the swallow dove. Wings back the swallow slipped from the sky to home in on its target. Three metres, two metres, one, a pink and blue form hove into sight, danger! The swallow wavered in its flight, but undeterred and calculating its trajectory to perfection, the swallow snatched up its prey and, carried by its own momentum, scooped its lithe form back into the sky and out of harm's way.

Surprised by the sudden blur of movement, as he wandered into the yard, George Penton stopped in his tracks. He peered into the sky following the bird's ascent and smiled to himself; the first swallow of spring, a sure sign that warmer and better times were on their way.

Idly wiping his hands on his blue-blotched overalls George's thoughts wandered back down to earth, and there his eyes were greeted by yet another surprise; outside his tractor shed, standing incongruously amongst the mud, and gleaming in the bright morning light, was a sleek black car.

At first, he could not see who the owner of this non-utilitarian vehicle could be, but then George noticed the stranger. Standing in the road and staring into the field the man was obviously absorbed in his thoughts. However, as George watched, the man's attention appeared to return from the distance and he turned his gaze upon George. Pushing himself away from the wall the stranger strode confidently across the concrete yard, neatly avoiding the steaming piles and, before George could gather his thoughts, the man was upon him.

"Hello," the stranger smiled, holding out his hand. "Allow me to introduce myself. John Dally." The name was pronounced in a manner that suggested that it was a noun to be remembered; a language teacher might well have told their student, "This is a chair," in much the same tone.

The farmer did not reply at first, nor offer his hand in greeting. He merely looked the man up and down, taking in the casual, but obviously expensive suit, and the man's carefully ruffled hair and sculptured stubble. This man was too casually groomed to be a feed rep, and too expensively clad to have anything to do with the Inland Revenue, even if they did take a fortune off him.

George slowly held his hand out in response. He knew it was covered in oil, but that was something this intruder would just have to bear with.

"George Penton," he said, pleasantly surprised that the man shook his hand firmly, with no sign of hesitation. "What can I do for you?"

"Well, I was hoping that you might be able to furnish me with some information," the man stuck his hands in his pockets—bulging the grey wool of the suit. He appeared relaxed and at ease, which was far more than George felt. "I've been looking at the stone in the field over there," he continued, "and I was wondering if it was your field and whether you knew anything of the stone's history?"

"You a tourist are you?" George asked, suspiciously.

"You might say that." the man smiled.

"Might I?" the farmer responded. "Well it is my field alright, but the stone's history is much longer than mine. It has been standing in that field for as long as my family has been living here. And that," he added with his usual pride, "is over three hundred years."

"Really?" the man replied, "Well I'd certainly like to know more about it. I'm very interested in that stone."

"Maybe you are and maybe you aren't," George responded brusquely, "but I can't tell you anymore than that. All I know is that it has been in my family for centuries, and for that reason we've kept it there. Makes us feel as though there's some permanence about the place." He pulled a bunch of keys from his pocket and hefted them in his broad heavy hand. "I'm sorry but that's all I can tell you. And now, if you will excuse me, I've got to get on with my work."

"No! Look," the man cried, "you don't understand. I'm interested in buying the stone."

Open Door

Jonathan slammed the heel of his hand into the hot air vent of the car. "Why the hell can't you get a car with a decent heater?" he stormed.

"The heater is fine," David said slowly and patiently, "it just needs a little time to warm up that's all."

"How much time can it need?" Jonathan sneered. "Perhaps we should have shown it yesterday's weather forecast. Then it would have known that fifty miles from Cornwall it would start to piss down, and could begin to prepare itself for the big event."

Pursing his lips, David stared fixedly ahead as he steered the car, and steeled himself for the explosion. "You're not really angry with the car," he said quietly, "you're angry with my mother."

It happened.

"Too bloody right I'm angry with your mother," Jonathan spat. "She and this car are ideally suited: the Ice Maiden and her mobile fridge. I'm going to have a few choice words to say to her when we arrive, I can tell you that for nothing."

"Well I wouldn't say anything just yet," David said, turning the blue Fiesta back onto the A30.

"Why not?" snapped Jonathan. "The old bag deserves to be told where to get off. For Christ's sake, she rings me up at four o' clock in the morning just to tell me to bring that picture of hers back; she could have waited until the morning."

"It was the morning."

"Don't get funny. You know what I mean."

"Maybe," David sighed, "but perhaps she thought we were going to be leaving terribly early, and was afraid of missing you."

"Perhaps, but I doubt it," Jonathan retorted, slumping back into his seat.

David drummed his fingers on the leather trim around the steering wheel and waited, but not for long.

"I mean to say," Jonathan complained, "I've got my agent on my back to finish off Per-verse, a director from hell, who thinks he's God and hashes up my plot every time he breathes, and I take time off to haul that monstrosity of hers around to be valued. 'Oh you have all the right connections' she said," he was really working himself up to full momentum now. "And then for her to turn around and say, 'I hope you've treated it well and haven't damaged it'. That battle-axe deserves to be told a few home truths. If I hadn't been so tired at the time I'd have told her too. I feel like putting my fist through the damn thing."

"I think that's rather lacking in style. Perhaps you should just paint a moustache on it," David speculated.

"Yes," Jonathan snarled. "Now that is an idea," he smiled deviously. "A nice big bristling sergeant major's moustache. I could use yours as the model."

"No," his friend mused, fingering his black, red flecked, bristles. "I don't think so; I think it needs to grow about another foot first."

"Or maybe just a toe," Jonathan chuckled.

David smiled; he knew his friend's mood had been broken.

Half an hour later, the car sped up the gravel driveway, and, approaching the house, executed what would have been a spectacular hand brake turn, were it not marred by the fact that the rear right wheel struck the doorstep.

David glanced out of his door to see if there was any damage to the wheel and then craned his neck to view the curve his turn had carved in the gravel. He smiled in satisfaction. "You can only do that sort of thing when your mother is the owner of the establishment. One of the perks of life," he said, still smiling as he jumped out of the car. "Come my friend, step lively now," he opened Jonathan's door with a theatrical bow. "And may I take the opportunity of welcoming you to the Twilight Boarding House."

"More like welcome to the Twilight Zone," murmured Jonathan, stooping as he stepped stiffly out. He stretched his long thin frame in the cold grey air and David could not help but wince as watched his friend regain his height advantage to the accompaniment of clicking joints.

"Come on," Jonathan said, reaching for the picture. "We might as well get on with it."

David tugged hard on the rusting wrought iron bell-pull, but there were no answering chimes to be heard issuing from the interior. Nevertheless, a moment later, the door was flung open and a mantis-like form exploded from the darkened doorway. "Darling!" it cried, flinging its thin, green clad arms around David's unresisting form, "How wonderful to see you, after all this time."

"So this is what it means by being taken back into the bosom of the family," Jonathan quietly observed as he watched his friend's head being plunged into the cleavage.

The Mantis looked up from the rapture of its reunion, and cast a vaguely disapproving, yet resigned eye, over the shoulder of her offspring.

"And Jonathan," her tone dropped as she disengaged herself from David. "How are you? You know you're not looking at all well; I do hope you're looking after yourself." She studied him speculatively, in much the same manner as his GP's receptionist studied all new patients, but her gaze came to rest on the picture. "Never mind," she continued more lightly. "We'll soon feed you up and set you back on your feet. But don't just stand there, come on in."

"Strange," muttered Jonathan to David, as she turned to lead the way down the hallway, "she already has me feeling fed up."

New Arrival

Green, grey, gold and white, were the colours that greeted the eye. The bleached white stones of the gravel path stood out from, and yet complimented, their surroundings, leading the viewer from the gate and through the short avenue of evergreens towards the grey stone backdrop of the house. However, barring the eye's rite of passage and partly masking the scene, was a bottle green lorry, its gold emblazoned sides flashing in the bright spring sunshine as it rocked in time to the ticking of its engine. The blurred and shuddering form of the lorry appeared to shrink in size as the engine was stilled and the motion ceased, allowing the gold lettering on its sides to resolve into the words 'Henry's Haulage'.

Henry himself was at the wheel, and he heaved a tired sigh of relief at having reached the end of a long, difficult and nerve wracking journey. Bending forward, he massaged the tense muscles at the back of his aching neck, coaxing black rolls of sweat soaked skin to peel off and lodge under his nails. The relief was minimal, but at least the journey was over.

The gravel crunched under his steel-capped boots, casting a thin white powder onto the brown broken leather, as Henry made his ponderous way towards the house with the intent of announcing his arrival. But he needn't have bothered—before he had even gained the steps, the gleaming white door was thrown open on its thick black hinges and a tall and ruffled young man came bounding down to greet him. Henry recognized the man as his temporary employer, John Dally.

No longer in a suit and well groomed, but clad in a baggy white shirt with rolled up sleeves, and wearing a two-day stubble, the man still exhibited the same enthusiasm, energy and exuberance which Henry found so disconcertingly unpredictable.

"You brought it then," the man said, throwing his arm around Henry's shoulders, and turning him back towards the cab. "No problems I hope?"

"No, not once we got going at any rate." Henry replied, casting a worried glance at the embracing arm.

"What do you mean, what happened?"

"Well my winch can handle almost anything, sir," he replied, pointing to the powerful crane in the back of his lorry. "But that rock of yours took a lot of shifting. When we tried to get it out of the ground, the whole front of the truck lifted up. To be honest, I didn't think we were going to make it."

"Well I'm very glad you did," John Dally's relief was obvious. "But I suppose everything else went okay?" he enquired absently, looking up at the stone. "No other problems I hope?"

"As a matter of fact there were, sir." The reproach in Henry's tone was clear, and he hoped that it was relayed to his employer; he was certain that John Dally had seriously underestimated the weight of the stone when he had first described the commission. "As I was driving off that rock of yours shifted position. Nearly tipped me over it did. It doesn't take much for a weight like that to upset your balance."

"No," Dally said vaguely as he stepped closer to study the stone above him, "I'm sure it doesn't. But, maybe that's exactly what it's meant to do.

"I'm sorry sir?"

"Oh nothing. But it wasn't damaged in any way was it?"

"No sir," Henry couldn't help chuckling in surprise. "If you ask me that's the thing that does the damaging."

"So that is what all the fuss has been about is it?"

Henry and John Dally turned around at the sound of the voice to see John's wife, Marian, coming towards them; her bob of short red hair, living up to its name as she bounced down the steps.

"Yes, darling," John said warmly, "that is what all the fuss has been about. Amazing isn't it?"

"It's certainly amazingly priced," she replied. "I don't know of any stones apart from those in Elizabeth Taylor's rings which have cost as much." Her slender white fingers brushed through her hair as she stood at the rear of the lorry, examining the stone. "But I have to agree with you," she nodded as she joined the others, "it does have a certain natural magnificence. I'm sure you can improve on it though, darling; with your own natural magnificence." She smiled up at her husband as she put her arms around his waist.

Henry, totally unembarrassed, watched with interest. "Well, sir," he said earnestly, "I only wish my wife had as much faith in me. No, I have to say, faith isn't something she has a lot of, but she can put the fear of God into me. Which is exactly what she'll do if I don't get home soon," he added with a wink at Marian. "So if you will just tell me where to drop this off I'll leave you to it."

"Of course," John said. "If you could just take it over there to my workshop. I have a trolley ready waiting for it."

The sight of John Dally walking away with his arm still around the slim waist of his wife brought the twinkle of a smile to Henry's eyes. A tinge of envy, he felt, might have been more appropriate for this pair who seemed to have everything, but they did seem like such a nice couple. It was nice to know that some people still lived in fairy tales, he thought happily, as he climbed back into his cab.

The lorry grumbled back into life, as Henry turned its key, and in preparation for disgorging its two and a half ton load, reversed towards the entrance of the workshop.

Stretched as tightly as a vocal cord, the creaking steel hawser spoke of the stone's weight and joined in a chorus of protest with the labouring winch and the truck's stressed suspension, as, having raised the stone, it began to lower it slowly over the side.

Revolving slowly on its tether, the stone resembled a huge elongated and rugged egg hanging crookedly from a thread as, inch-by-inch, it was lowered into position—albeit the wrong position.

Blast!" John cursed. "It's off centre."

His breath steamed into the clutch of the crisp spring air as, to no avail, he braced his own meagre poundage against that of the stone in an attempt to guide its decent.

Seeing her husband's predicament, and thinking more along the lines of moving Mohammed to the Mountain, Marian stepped forward and attempted to edge the trolley further beneath the stone.

Crack!

Whether it was the winch giving way or the suspension, the effect was the same. The stone suddenly dropped by several inches, its angled base striking the edge of the trolley and flipping the solid frame away with the nonchalant ease of a giant tiddlywink.

Marian hurled herself to the side, but still, the heavy steel structure slammed into her shin with a vicious blow that sent her sprawling to the ground. Pushing hard, but caught off guard by the sudden movement, John slipped from the stone, a huge gout of life scented breath punching up into the air as bruised, stunned and winded he crashed backwards onto the hard ground. Slamming on the brake Henry stopped the winch; but the damage had already been done. He looked down on two motionless figures: a mighty sword of Damocles swinging between them in the form of the tethered stone.

Centre stage, on a thick block of Elm, the stone completely dominated its surroundings within the white walled studio. Even with his back turned to the monolith, John felt that he could sense the stone's presence permeating to every corner of the room. However, its impact on his senses was far more than the merely ethereal; it was also physical. The stone was large; just over nine feet eleven inches in height: nearly ten feet or three or thirty hands. John looked at the tape measure in his hands as he stepped off the ladder; an interesting size he thought, and as for its circumference, that was interesting too. But, perhaps girth would be a better term to describe it? Yes, its girth. It was just under eight feet eight inches, twenty-six hands or two hundred and sixty six centimetres. Just as its height had been an almost perfectly symmetrical figure, its girth was the very antithesis.

"Still admiring your acquisition then?"

It was Marian, who had entered behind him, her walking stick's rubber tip making a slight squeak on the tiled floor.

"Hmm, well, not so much admiring, although it is admirable, but rather contemplating it."

"And what, exactly, were you contemplating, my vexed and brilliant sculptor?" There was almost a shade of sarcasm in her voice, but John knew her better. She merely coloured her tone to stifle his conceit and to retain her self-respect. He flickered a brief smile in response to the compliment.

"If you must know, my darling, I was just trying to get some idea of its function and history. Look at the top, for example, it's obvious that it has already been crafted by hands much older than mine. You can see the marks where the stone has been chipped away. And that can't have been an easy job."

"How do you know that?"

"Because, although many of the standing stones in this country are sand stone, this happens to be granite, and 'as hard as granite' is a very telling simile." He paused and looked at his wife accusingly. "Unlike 'as tough as old boots', which is how you described my steak."

"Oh it was a bootiful steak darling," Marian said, mockingly. "Really bootiful."

"Hmmph," John snorted. "I don't know; I try to care for my ailing wife by giving vent to my creative culinary flair, and what happens? I get my efforts thrown back in my face."

"So that's what it was. I thought that some sort of flare must have gone off in the kitchen, judging by all the smoke. Anyway, I didn't throw your steak back in your face; it might have killed you."

"Very droll."

"Oh don't sulk," Marian said, prodding him in the ribs with her stick. "Tell me more about your stone. Is granite always the same morbid colour?"

"No," he replied. "Actually it isn't," he patted the stone defensively. "In fact it varies quite a lot; ranging from black, like this, to light grey, or from pale pink to red."

"The pink sounds nice," Marian commented, "but how did they manage to carve it if it was so hard?"

"To be honest I'm not sure, but I do know when you're trying to guide me onto my pet topic."

"Who me?"

"Yes, you. But, anyway, I also know that the Egyptians used to carve out massive blocks of granite by hitting them with a slightly harder piece. The main effect of this was to create a lot of dust, but, if teams of hundreds of men kept hitting the rock, then eventually, the rock was worn away to the shape they wanted, or more accurately the shape, their masters wanted. There were whole villages close to the pyramids just inhabited by the craftsmen and their families, and it is even on record that they were the ones to have the first reported strike." Walking around the stone, he ran his hand over its surface, his thoughts drifting back to the days of the Stone Age masons. A thought occurred to him. He stopped, and peered around the stone at his wife. His voice brightened. "We, sometimes, still use a similar system to theirs today, but we always use a condom for protection."

"What!"

He laughed, "What we do is we place rubber over those parts of the stone which we want to protect and then sand-blast the rest; after which we use emery wheels for the details."

"Oh." Marian sounded relieved. "Don't you use chisels at all then?"

"Yes, but it is hard work. Granite is harder than marble, and you need a really hard point to make any impression on it. It's heavy too: one hundred and twenty to one hundred and forty pounds per cubic foot. But, what makes it even harder to work is the fact that it's so brittle; one wrong tap with a point and a whole section could flake off. I'm quite worried about it."

There was a pause befitting the fate of a lost flake.

"So you're saying that some extremely determined prehistoric sculptor got there before you."

"Yes they did that alright, and then they placed it, totally isolated, in the middle of a field. Mind you, having said that, it wasn't entirely isolated. I later found out that there was another stone standing across the river from this one. But it wasn't nearly so large or impressive."

"Well I'm glad you didn't try to buy that one as well. We would have had to sell the house to afford it."

"Yes I know," John sighed. "I'm sorry that it cost so much, but there was no way he was going to sell it otherwise. It had been on his family's land for generations, and it was only because he'd had a health scare with his stock that he agreed to the sale. Not only did he need to buy new stock, but he wanted to replace the building as well."

"With the amount you gave him he could have bought a new house besides," Marian commented wryly. "I just hope that what ever you decide to do with the thing, that it makes your money back for you."

"That's just it," John said, turning away from his wife. "I'm not sure that I am going to do anything with it."

"What!" Marian exclaimed.

"Well!" John rejoined, "It's just that when I saw it standing there in the field it looked so natural." He turned back and revealed a face that was fighting for words and understanding. His voice lowered. "It was a part of nature, placed there as a statement by some ancient man, and I thought I wanted to take it and show it to the world. I wanted everyone to be a witness to that statement. But now that I've removed it from its original site, the statement seems to have changed."

"What do you mean?"

"Well it looked so in harmony before, man's work with nature, because it was set in a natural environment. Now, in here, and where ever it is going to be set, it won't have the same effect. Man's work within man's work." He paused. "It looked so different with the rain running down it."

"Then perhaps you should make it into a fountain." Marian suggested.

John turned slowly towards his wife and stared at her, his eyes wide with excitement and realization.

"That could just be it," he said. "You are amazing. I have been standing here, my brain so clouded with awe of the thing, that I couldn't see the obvious. I will have to find someone willing to commission a fountain, but that shouldn't be too difficult, and I'll have to work out where I'm going to cut the water channels, but in the end, I'll dress the stone and redress the balance. Ha. Water and stone, man and nature could soon be reunited.

"You know I think I might go climbing with Roger this weekend, it might help me to get some ideas." He looked down on his wife, picked her up, stick and all, and swung her round in a wide arc. "Oh, what would I do without you?"

Empty Fields

A grunt rumbled from between the lips of George Penton, as he sat at the long, pine kitchen table, a mug of coffee in hand. The information in the letter, spread in front of him, did not become any more palatable with further reading. The Council wanted to convert the small, 'B' road into a dual carriageway, "In order to cope with the increasing tourist traffic" so it said, but dual carriageways didn't like to turn corners, and, as a result, they wanted to take it across his land. Very close to his house in fact.

Getting up, George slowly paced towards the kitchen window overlooking the field. Without the stone, the field seemed bare, but he'd had to sell it to save the farm; and now others were trying to take part of his farm from him. His father had always said to him, in what seemed like a cliché now: "Everything comes from the land son, and everything goes back to it. We've got a part of that land. Never let it go," and now here he was being forced to give up some of that very land by a bunch of stupid, little officials. Well he wasn't going to let it happen. What would Harry say; he didn't even know about the stone yet, and when he found out about this latest development, he would hit the roof.

In anguish, George continued to look out across the field, and wished that the stone were still there—it used to help him think. He would go down to the pub tonight, he decided, maybe his friends could help him where the stone could not.

The wheel squeaked slightly as George pulled the bike away from the wall. Reaching up he got the small oilcan down from the shelf and pumped some of its contents onto the bearings; he took a pride in all of his machines, and he was not going to roll into town sounding like a wheezing crate.

The evening was very warm, which was why George had decided on this particular mode of transport, and, as he pedalled slowly past his fields, he regarded them with warm pride; an emotion which always laid claim to him whenever he had time to contemplate his property—property on which others had now laid their covetous gaze. The thought washed away his pride with waves of anger on a creeping tide of guilt. No one was going to take his farm from him. He bent his thickset form and pushed hard on the peddles, flying past and away from his fields as though fleeing from their judgement.

Two miles further on, as the lights of the village came into sight, George slowed his pace. He was hardly even breathless, which he felt to be quite good going for a man of fifty-two. Working on a farm, he always said, was the ideal way to keep in shape. Admittedly, that shape, in his case, was a little round, but, as he said to the girls, it was just enough to keep two people warm. Without doubt, his throbbing muscles felt warm enough for two people as he dismounted from his bike and this increased his desire for a pint into an urgent need.

Having to stoop as he passed through the Crown's black oak door, George stepped into an atmosphere which many mockingly rustic bars tried, and failed to emulate, through plastic pretensions and multitudes of redundant horse brasses. Not one gleaming agricultural implement adorned the walls and the scarred oaken beams were warped with the weight of ages, not by the attentions of the forger's craft.

Tucked out of the way of the tourist routes the scene within this time capsule had changed with the seasons, but not with the years. Clothes and conversations revolved around the dictates of nurturing and reaping the land's harvest and the practicalities of that purpose had hardly changed with the centuries; the tools had merely become more efficient. And so, as the seasons pulsed around the outside of the Crown's flaking white walls, and time flowed by, the Crown's interior maintained its own rhythm in time to the ebb and flow of the fire in the grate. For here, the fire only went out at night, along with the customers; burning low in summer and high in winter, providing a focal point for those without a companion with which to share a conversation and a source of heat and light to those who needed to rid their bones of a chill. Now, in early spring, it was already on the ebb—casting out a flickering orange glare from its position behind the door across the bare boards towards the darkly polished bar and catching the motes of dust and smoke along its path to turn each into a glittering reflection of itself. But, behind this band of burnished copper, lay an even brighter strip of gold, for beyond the fire the sluggish rays of the setting sun were bursting through the small open window and competing with the fire for dominance over this usually murky room. As a result, the overall impression was one of a room filled with the misty incandescence of the Milky Way, seen through the rose coloured glasses or bloodshot eyes of the avid drinker, and there, in its midst, sat a hunched figure. Framed and unmoving, he almost appeared to be part of the room itself, set in his place along with the foundations.

"Hello Lad, how are you?" George asked, slapping the man on the back.

The object of George's attention, a small thin man, in his late seventies, rocked from the impact of George's friendly pat. The title of 'Lad', connected to such a frail old man, may have seemed absurd to outsiders, but his employer at Thorn Hill Farm had bestowed it upon him before the war, and, now its attachment to him was stronger than that of his thinning grey hair.

Spilt beer glistened on the thin skin of the old man's hand as, still recovering; he turned to look up at the burly farmer. "Oh I'm grand George," his thin voice crackled, "all the better for seeing you."

"That's fine. You'll be having another of those then?" George asked, indicating the beer glass in Lad's hand.

"Oh you know me George," he replied, chuckling.

"I do Lad, I do that," George smiled. "Well then, my beauty," he called to the barmaid as he strode to the counter. "I'll have two pints of your finest please, and one for yourself of whatever takes your fancy, as long as it's me." He winked at the woman, who smiled coyly in return as she went to pour the beers. "Will you look at her," George continued, addressing the bar in general. "She's a joy to watch. Poetry in motion. Just look at those muscles rising as she pulls those pints. You could crack walnuts between muscles like that."

But it wasn't her muscles that George was watching, and, as she returned with the drinks, he leant over the bar to stare at the small gold medallion, hanging between the cleavage exposed above her white, stretched T-shirt.

"What is that?" he asked, lowering his voice and his gaze.

"It's my good luck charm."

"Well, Linda, I'll tell you something, it's bloody lucky to be there. Do you think I'll ever be able to charm my way into its place?"

Looking into his eyes, and with slow deliberation, Linda leant towards him, placing her palm over the money he had left on the counter. "You never know George," she whispered in his ear, "you never know." She winked in return and slid the money into her hand as she turned back to the till.

George raised his eyebrows and took a quick gulp of his drink, there was hope yet, there was most definitely hope. A small self-congratulatory smile crept across his face as he picked up his drinks and walked over to Lad's table. "There you go Lad," he said, setting the glass down. "Now don't you go drinking it down all at once," and, with that, he made his way towards the corner table, where a group of three men were lolling in relaxed discussion.

"Hello chaps," George greeted. "Need any refills?"

A tall, distinguished man with sweptback hair glanced up, "No thanks George," he replied, "Barney here has just bought a round."

"Fine, I'll get the next one then. I'll just sit down and take the weight off my feet. I cycled here; it being such a great night."

"Aye, it's a fine evening all right," said Barney, shifting his chair to make room for George, "but you'll soon be able to buy one of those open top sports cars with the money you got from that stone of yours."

George looked at Barney's darkly freckled face under its mass of curly black hair and, not for the first time, thought; Dennis the Menace.

"Oh yes," George laughed, to cover his smile."I can just see me now, driving along the Champs Elysees with Linda there beside me; her hair streaming in the wind, the flies sticking to our pearly white teeth."

The others laughed.

"But I'll tell you lads," George continued in more sombre tone, "my problems with the farm haven't finished yet, and I don't think money is going to help me this time."

"Why what's the matter?" the tall man asked.

"Actually, Gerry, that's what I wanted to speak to you about. The council have sent me a letter. It seems that they want to take part of my field away from me, in order to build a new road."

"Christ! You do have your problems don't you?" Gerry exclaimed, setting his glass down with a thud.

"Which field do they want?" Barney asked, as he and the others pulled their chairs in around the table.

"It's the south field, the same one as the stone was in," George replied. "They want to run a dual carriageway through one corner of it. To improve the road for the tourist trade, so they say."

"Well I'm not really the person you should be talking to," Gerry said, shaking his head. "I'm only a Librarian. Didn't the council give you someone to contact, or haven't you got a solicitor you can consult?"

"They gave me a name in the letter, Heather Mason, but what's the point in talking to them, they're the ones after my land."

"Well at least you will be able to find out exactly what they want. Have you got the letter here with you?"

"Yes, here it is." George threw the letter over.

Picking up the letter, Gerry carefully unfolded it and turned to allow the light from the window to illuminate the words. He read slowly whilst the others watched in silence. Eventually he refolded the letter and handed it back. "You should get some pretty decent compensation out of them anyway," he commented.

George tossed the letter over to Barney. "I don't want compensation, I want my land," he snapped.

Mike, the fourth member of the group spoke up. "You know they might not have to take your land. They could go over it; build a bridge. I heard of one farmer who made them give him a bridge, just so he could bring his cattle safely over the road for milking."

"No that would be no good for me either," George said. "I use that field for grazing; it's the only thing I can use it for with the stones being in there and it being so damp. Can you imagine what could happen to my milk yield if I had a dual carriageway going over the top of my herd? I'll tell you what would happen, it'd drop right off."

"Then," Gerry said, "I think the best thing that you can do is get in touch with this Heather Mason and find out exactly what they want. Do not accept anything right away, and get in touch with your solicitor. You're going to need a bloody good excuse to get out of handing over your field to the greater good of the community. The only thing that normally does it is if you can prove you've got a site of outstanding beauty or some endangered species there. It's a pity you got rid of that stone of yours."

"Yes I was thinking that earlier," a morose George replied.

Stones In The Grass

To Jonathan's eye the interior of the spacious kitchen would have provided the perfect setting for a period drama, as everything about the room suggested the late Victorian or early Edwardian era. The props were all there; the large open fire, now lying grey and exhausted, dominating the east wall, the long deal table holding centre stage, and the white enamelled Aga stove resting against the whitewashed west wall and heating the huge pan of fragrant, frying, bacon. Soft light bathed the scene, splashed with bursts of bronzed brilliance from the rows of highly burnished copper pans, which hung in front of the large leaded windows, and splattered the rays from the early spring sun around the low kitchen as if they were a bronzed Mirror Ball.

Jonathan rested quietly against the Welsh Dresser by the door, whilst David quickly and confidently gathered the cups saucers and tea service from the drawers and cupboards. Idly watching David and his mother bustling around the kitchen, Jonathan realized, that David had returned home—a place that laid claim to David's youth and held his past, and a place that he, himself, knew only as a fleeting visitor and an outsider to its homely familiarity and routines.

"Well boys," David's mother said as she turned away from putting the kettle on the stove, "how long did you say you were intending to stay?"

"Oh about three weeks," David loftily replied. "I thought it would be a great opportunity to return to my roots and see my native land in all its spring bedecked glory."

"Really?" his mother said, raising an eyebrow. "And is your business doing so well that you can afford to leave it for three weeks?"

"I certainly hope so, and besides, I know that accounts and tax returns don't pine for me in the way that you do."

"Hmm. And what about you Jonathan," she asked, her sharp eyes slicing round, "have you nothing better to do?"

"Oh you'd be surprised Mrs Pengelly," Jonathan returned with a wry smile. "You really would be surprised."

"I doubt it Jonathan," her voice had the edge of a mantrap. "I think I'm past being surprised or shocked by the things that other people do." The glare that locked onto Jonathan almost made him quail, and it was a sensation that was neither familiar nor appreciated. He gulped with relief when he saw her eyes and demeanour soften; perhaps she was going to show compassion to her cowering foe. Perhaps. She selected one of the wooden high backed kitchen chairs and held it out for her guest.

"But what am I doing by not offering you a seat?" she asked with honeyed voice. "Please, do sit down."

Having no real option, but to accept the proffered seat, Jonathan settled back, only to catch a blazing shaft of sunlight, dancing from a gleaming pan, straight in his eye. He bowed his head and sighed, he felt that it was going to be a very long three weeks.

Carrying his plate through, Jonathan was surprised to see that the small dining room was already filling with guests. Selecting a table next to the bay windows he sat down, waiting for David to join him. He did not have to wait long, but unfortunately when David did appear Mrs Pengelly was in tow and loudly berating her son.

"And I do hope that you're going to do something about those bikes of yours soon," she said, dogging David's steps, "because if you don't then I will."

Jonathan sniffed the air as the two protagonists came towards him. "Excuse me Mrs Pengelly," he ventured.

"Not now Jonathan; I am talking to David."

Jonathan knew when he was beaten, and getting up, he walked away from the embarrassingly loud argument, and into the kitchen, to investigate the acrid smell that had called for his attention.

Returning through the breakfasting guests, to report to David's mother, Jonathan fought hard to hide his smirk from view. "Excuse me, Mrs Pengelly." he tried.

"Jonathan," came the snapped retort, "I am having a conversation with David, and I consider it rather rude of you to interrupt, what is, a family discussion. Now if you will just wait, I will attend to you in a moment." Flinging a look of exasperation at the interested guests she resumed her attack on David, until finally, her grievances aired, she turned her attention back to the young man hovering at her shoulder. "Now Jonathan what can I do for you? More tea?"

"No thank you Mrs Pengelly. Your toaster's on fire."

Jonathan and David pulled off their small backpacks and sat down on the grassy slope of the hill rising behind them.

"You should really have done something to try and put out the fire you know," David said.

"Oh it was alright," Jonathan replied, "I saw that there was nothing near it. Anyway she should have a smoke alarm fitted; fire and brimstone can never be far away from your mother."

"Come on that's not fair. She's had a tough time."

"Is that any reason for her to give everyone else one too?"

"I don't think it is everyone else."

"Just me, thanks. Remind me to leave her out of my Christmas card list."

"She sent you one last year."

"Yes, and look what it was. Where the hell, and I use that word advisedly, did she manage to get a Christmas card depicting Dante's Inferno?"

"She thought it was artistic."

"She thought it depicted my future."

"Oh stop, you're becoming paranoid. Eat your sandwiches."

Jonathan took a bite from his sandwich and almost immediately spat it out on the grass.

"Garlic! The cow," he cried.

"What's the matter?" David asked.

Jonathan was pulling his sandwich apart and examining it. "She's given me a cheese sandwich with garlic mayonnaise, that's what's wrong."

"That was what you asked for wasn't it?"

"No. What I asked for was a cheese sandwich with mayonnaise. And, when she asked what cheese I wanted, I said Cheddar, as I didn't like strong flavours, and she's gone and put garlic mayonnaise all over it!"

"She must have got the jars mixed up."

"I don't think so," said Jonathan, peering into his sandwich. "Look you can see lumps of garlic. She's planted them!"

"Now you are being paranoid," David said. "Look have my sandwich, it's roast beef and tomato. I'll have yours."

They swapped sandwiches, and ate in comparative silence, until Jonathan pointed down the hill:

"What's that stone over there?" he asked, "by the river."

"It's a standing stone," David responded. "As far as I know it's always been there. But that is a point," his voice sounded puzzled, "there used to be another stone as well; on the other side of the river. I wonder where it could have gone to?"

"We could try and find out," Jonathan suggested. "It will give us a purpose to our walk."

David slowly rose to his feet, his eyes still searching the landscape for the missing stone, "Okay," he agreed. "Come on."

Packing up their gear, they slung their backpacks onto their shoulders and set off down the hill, with David in the lead.

Crossing the road, they hurriedly checked that they were unobserved and jumped across a gap in the wall into the field. Less cautious now that they had a barrier between themselves and the road they set off across the grass bearing right towards the river.

As Jonathan strode through the long grass with his head bowed, the warm scent rose from the stems to meet his appreciative nose. Their rich perfume billowed around him with contours as precise and clear as the coloured bands of a rainbow, and then, from their midst, arose a sense of loss. Cloying, heavy and yet empty it impregnated his thoughts, laid claim to his consciousness and left him alone. He was standing by the bed, holding the cold hand of his dead grandfather, looking through blurred eyes as his mother left him on his first day at school, listening to the sound of his brother's feet as he walked away, locked in the dark cellar. He was alone, he was empty, he was nothing.

Like a credit card in the hands of a thief opening a lock, a familiar voice slipped through the void, opened a door and pulled him out. "What's the matter? Are you alright?"

"I don't ..," Jonathan shook his head in bewilderment, and looked up at his friend. "I think someone just walked over my grave." He lowered his head once more and scanned his surroundings. There, at his feet, shaped like a partly buried Ostrich egg, was a stone, about six inches in height, concealed in the grass, and it gripped his attention so intensely that his eyes watered with the pain of staring.

David came over and followed his friend's gaze, "Actually," he commented, "it's very like the missing stone, except smaller of course. Strange that you should have found it like that though."

"Strange is the right word," said Jonathan, "I felt like I'd suddenly been dumped in a deep freezer and someone had thrown away the key."

"A brush with the paranormal eh? You'll be seeing Jan Tregeagle next. Never mind let's see if we can find its big brother."

"Who is Jan Tregeagle?"

"A local ghost and ex magistrate. Come on."

They walked on, but it was only a few steps later that Jonathan again felt the faint traces of the mind numbing tendrils reaching into his mind. "I think there is something just over here," he muttered. He veered off to his left, trying to shake the intrusive sensation, as slowly and cautiously he traced its path. He stopped. There at his feet was yet another stone. He walked on and found another stone and then another and realised that he was walking in a circle that must be a few hundred feet in diameter.

"Come over here." It was David calling to him from, what appeared to be, the riverbank and, walking over, Jonathan noticed that David seemed to be alternately studying the sun and his watch.

"Look," called David, as he drew near. "This is where the stone was, it's been pulled out of here like an old tooth. The ground hasn't even healed over yet. It was at the head of the circle and in a direct line with the stone across the river pointing south west."

Jonathan peered down into the dark jagged hole, "Don't they normally mark stone circles on the maps?" he asked.

"Yes they do, but maybe, because it's hidden in the grass, they didn't know about this one. I didn't even find out about it until several years after we moved here."

"Who do you suppose moved the stone?" Jonathan asked.

"Presumably the farmer who owns the land. I can think of a couple of good reasons why he would want to be rid of it."

"Oh yes, and what are those?"

David looked away towards the farmhouse, "Oh nothing," he answered vaguely, "it doesn't matter, but the farmer must know what happened to the stone—he knows about most things that happen round here, he's quite a character. His name is George Penton, a good Cornish name."

"What makes it a good Cornish name?" Jonathan asked.

"By Tre, Pol and Pen. Ye may know the Cornish men," David replied. "It also goes for the place names."

"You mean like Penzance?"

"Yes. Pen means headland or promontory, so Penzance means holy headland. Tre is similar. It means hamlet, so Tremaine means hamlet at the stone."

"You're a mine of information."

"Thank you.

"Shall we see if we can find this good Cornish man?"

It was with some relief that Jonathan jumped back across the wall onto the road, thankfully leaving the indistinct sensation of loss behind him in the field. He walked towards the farmhouse "Which door shall we try?" he asked.

"I don't think either would be appropriate," David replied. "Like most farmers, he would probably take it as an insult that you expected to find him indoors at this time of day."

"What about his wife?"

"She died some years ago, a very devoted couple they were too, but it doesn't stop him from trying to play the field now. As I said he's quite a character."

They went round to the side of the house and into the yard, only to hear a loud curse emanating from one of the buildings. They walked towards the source of the voice and Jonathan saw a burly middle-aged man clad in blue overalls coming towards them with a series of rubber and metal pipes over his shoulder. The man stopped: "Hello," he said, "its David Pengelly isn't it? I heard you were in town."

"Ah, news travels as quickly as ever. George I would like you to meet my friend Jonathan Moseley."

"Pleased to meet you I'm sure."

"Likewise," Jonathan replied, shaking hands.

Out of the blue sky a throbbing pulse boomed towards them and halted their conversation with its intrusion. A helicopter beat its way over the house, reached the river, and the stone, and then headed east. David waited until its drone had died away before turning back to the farmer.

"George, we were wondering if you had any time to tell us what happened to that stone of yours, the one that used to be in your field over there?"

George raised an eyebrow, "Strange, now it's gone it's getting far more attention than when it was here. You never miss something until it's gone eh?

"Well, as it happens, I do have a bit of time to spare, so come on into the house, we'll have some tea and I'll get this cluster seen to as well."

"Thanks for your time George," David said as they were taking their leave. "We didn't think that stone could just have walked out of here. We'll probably see you in the Crown this evening."

"I'll look forward to that lads. Glad I could help."

George followed them out of the door and looked thoughtfully across his field. He had always felt that somehow the stone circle was connected to his old stone house. Maybe it was because he had broken the circle that he was having so much bad luck recently. It was his fault, after all, as David had said, the stone could not have walked away by itself, but, and now here was a thought, maybe it could walk back.

"Did you have a nice walk boys?" Mrs Pengelly asked on their return.

"Yes. Great," David replied. "We went over to George Penton's place and had a chat."

"Oh that's nice. Is he well?" his mother asked.

"Yes, he seems fine."

"That's good. Well I'd better go and get the dinner on then."

"And if you'll excuse me," Jonathan said, starting up the hallway, "I'll just have a quick shower before we eat. Oh by the way," he added, turning round. "Thank you for the cheese and garlic sandwiches, Mrs Pengelly. Garlic is meant to keep vampires away isn't it? That surely can't be true."

Mrs Pengelly turned to glare at Jonathan's retreating back.

Tumble

John Dally stood back and allowed his eyes to rove over the grey jagged rock face, following its contours and picking out a route on its time-etched features.

"We'll try this one shall we?"

Roger tightened the band around his grey ponytail and looked up speculatively towards the peak. "A bit easy isn't it?" he commented. "Do you want to go for a walk or a climb?"

"I'm not just here for fun you know. This is business as well; I'm trying to get my thoughts together man," John quipped, fingers raised in a peace sign.

"Oh I'm sorry," said Roger. "I should have known that there would be some greater purpose behind the great artist's and my mentor's actions. You scale those heights, oh master, and I, poor plebeian that I am, shall stand below and watch you ascend into the heavens, in awe of your blessed pilgrimage."

"Bollocks. You just make sure that I don't fall out of the heavens. Because if I do I'm going to fall on your face, which might just ruin sixteen years of friendship; although, I could carve you a brilliant coffin."

"Gee, thanks. And would I be allowed to design your eternal resting place if you were to come of worst?"

"Of course."

"Good, because, let's face it, you wouldn't need a particularly big one after that fall, you'd practically fit in a glass. I could call you 'Artist on the rocks'. What do you think?"

"I think you've got a warped mind, and I'm not sure that I want to go up there anymore."

"Oh come on. Where are your guts?"

"Inside me thank you, and I'd prefer it if they stayed there. As it is their contents don't feel too stable."

"Well you'll be alright going up there. It's more of a step ladder than a climb."

"Yes, I guess you're right. And it might help give me some ideas about what to do with this damn stone of mine."

"Oh I know. As I'm always saying to the wife, 'there is nothing like getting your hands on a nice rounded promontory for bringing your thoughts together'."

"Yes I bet you do."

"Seriously though," Roger said, "This sculpture of yours has really got you on edge hasn't it?"

"It's not so much the sculpture, but the stone itself. Maybe it is because I paid out so much for it that I'm feeling the pressure of having to justify my action. But, somehow, I think it's more than that—I don't know what it is, I can't explain it, the damn thing just unsettles me, but one thing I do know—it possesses amazing potential, and I don't know what to do with it."

"Well I hope this helps you figure it out," Roger said earnestly. He smiled: "But enough of this idle gossip. I've got the rope, you've got the mission, there's the cliff. Go get it, killer."

John grinned, "Okay, let's do it."

They moved to the base of the cliff. Roger, the rope coiled in his hands, scanned upwards. "But don't be too confident," he warned, "it was raining quite hard last night and it could be a bit slippery."

"Don't worry, I'll be careful," John replied, slotting his hands into the first holds of the climb.

Fifteen feet up and John took out the first of his pitons and hammered it into a small crack in the rock, like a knife into an open wound. He smiled to himself; it reminded him of preparing a stone by using a chisel to remove the spawl.

In clipping the rope through the piton, he noticed that it felt cold and damp. He withdrew his hands and looked down. Drops of red-flecked water were running out along the piton from where he had hammered it into the rock. Looking into, and up, the crevice he saw that a thin stream of water was trickling down onto the piton where it then ran out along its length.

"Christ," John swore softly to himself. "I thought it was bleeding for a moment. That would have been something to tell Marian about."

"Mrs Dally, Mrs John Dally?"

"Yes."

"May I come in? I have some information regarding your husband."

Marian looked at the W.P.C. and then past her to the male police officer standing by the car. "What is it?" she asked. "Is something wrong?"

"May I come in?"

"Yes, yes of course. Come through." Marian led the way through into the lounge. "What's the matter?" she asked again, propping herself on the mantelpiece.

"I'm afraid your husband has had a climbing accident."

"Is he alright?"

"No I'm afraid not. Mrs Dally I'm sorry to have to tell you that your husband died from his injuries."

Marian gripped hold of the mantelpiece so tightly that even through the mist that shot through her mind she could hear her nails cracking against the rag-rolled paintwork. However, it was not tight enough and, even as the thickening cloud continued to roll in, she could feel herself slipping, uncontrollably, downwards. An arm went round her waist, and she was lowered onto the sofa.

John. A picture of him and all that he meant to her pushed aside the consolatory shrouds trying to surround her. "What happened?" she asked.

"You just fainted for a moment."

"I don't mean that," Marian snapped. "I mean what happened to John?"

"I'm sorry. He fell from the cliff. Apparently, it was from a considerable height. He must have died immediately."

"What about Roger, is he alright?"

"Yes. He was on the ground. He wanted to come and see you himself, but I'm afraid he is still being treated for shock. He said that all the safety devices your husband used, Pitons I believe he called them, failed and slipped. It doesn't appear to have been anybody's fault."

Marian covered her face with her hands.

"Is there anyone we can get to stay with you?"

"My mother doesn't live far away."

"Do you want me to ring her?" the policewoman asked.

"No it's alright, I'll do it." Marian rose with determination and slowly dialled her old home. However, when she heard her mother's voice, the reality of the situation refused denial and slammed into her composure. She broke down and wept.

The policewoman gently took the receiver out of Marian's hand, placed an arm around her, and quietly explained the situation to Marian's mother.

On The Move

The tractor started with a cough, which quickly turned into a low rumble as it stood shaking on the concrete floor of the shed. George slipped the clutch and the machine eased its way forward into the night. With quick precision he turned the tractor and backed it towards the carefully prepared trailer. Nothing on there would rattle tonight—it had all been meticulously strapped down, and, if everything went according to plan, the trailer's contents would help him to achieve the greatest engineering feat he had ever attempted, and, in the process, save his farm.

George closed the shed door and climbed back onto his tractor. Standing on its seat, he scanned the surrounding valley. No telltale lights, so much for the increased tourist traffic—there could not be any cars for miles around, well he wasn't going to use any lights either. For tonight silence and darkness, the poacher's allies, were also his; he could reduce the noise, but he could eliminate the light.

The tractor followed the dirt track out of the yard and into the large field adjoining that which contained the circle. Once through the gate he turned right and continued slowly across the field, heading south and aiming for the gap in the wall.

The sound of the trailer bouncing into the water was quite loud, but here he was surrounded by his own land, and there should have been no one there to listen. Turning right once more, he pushed the tractor slowly upstream, its huge ribbed wheels beating through the eighteen inches of water and biting into the riverbed; blending the earth and the water into a dark foam. George looked back, the silt was already settling out. He smiled; let the buggers try to find my tracks under that lot he thought.

The stone was opposite him now, on the left bank, it looked even bigger from his position in the river. A doubt touched his resolve—was it too big? Sod it, nothing ventured, nothing gained. He turned the engine off and pulled up his waders, quickly going through the plan in his mind as he did so. It had seemed plausible enough on paper; he could only hope it proved to be so in practice.

Slipping down into the water, he waded downstream to unpack the trailer. The first thing he removed was a large spade, and with this in hand, he picked out a large sac and waded back up river. Walking up to the stone, he started to dig two straight lines directly in front of it and excavated the earth between them to a depth of about six inches; all the earth from which he carefully placed in a large sac. This finished, he placed some of the earth from the sac along the edges of the trench, in a pattern similar to those he had observed when ploughing his fields. Being careful to walk in a direct line from the stone to the river, George returned to ready the cables attached to the winches on the back of his tractor.

Collecting a couple of saddles from the trailer, he slung them over his shoulders and carried them, and the cables, back to the bank. Where, after strapping the saddles into position on the stone, he carefully settled the cables over their thickly padded seats in the hope of preventing any marks or scars being left on the rock surface.

Spade in hand, George again walked back into the water and began to dig a small pit in the riverbed; this would be the site for the pulleys that George had made. The pulleys consisted of an iron girder, five feet in length upon which two steel pulleys and a housing had been welded at one end, while the other end of the girder was sunk into the riverbed.

George led the cables up from the tractor to the top of the pulleys and then down onto the stone.

Taking a bucket from the trailer George then filled it with water and poured its contents into the ditch he had dug in front of the stone; creating a perfect mud slide. Now for the final stage: he started up the tractor and proceeded to reel in the cables. The bottom cable became taut first, and this had two effects. Firstly, it pushed the girder further into the riverbed, and, secondly, it pulled the bottom edge of the stone slightly proud of the ground. Before it could tip backwards, however, the top cable became taut and took the weight of the stone's peak. The stone then started to move very slowly forward, along the channel that George had cut for it. When it reached the end of this channel George kept pulling on the top cable, to bring the stone level, and stopped the motor. Taking his sack of earth back up to the stone, he placed its contents both in front and slightly along its width to disguise the channel. This completed he untied the cables and saddles and returned them to the trailer.

As he was scuffing dirt into the hole left by the girder George thought how surprisingly easy it had been to move this stone compared to trying to move the other one. Never mind, the important thing was that it had moved. Now all he had to do was to think of a way of advertising the fact.

The morning reflected George's mood: a thin grey mist lay over the fields, but on the horizon a bright sun was rising. He allowed himself the luxury of leaning on the gate as he stifled a yawn and let the cows traipse back into the field from the milking parlour. He was happy, or maybe he was merely optimistic, which was something he had not been for a long time. His plan had worked, it had physically exhausted him, but it was a good feeling and it had worked. He had pitted his own strength and ingenuity against the seemingly insurmountable forces of nature and he had won. Not only that but his cowhand had arrived on time this morning, the cluster he had repaired was working well and he had finished the milking in plenty of time for the aggressive punctuality of the milk tanker. God was in his heaven and for once, he wasn't throwing thunderbolts of misfortune down on him.

A familiar 'thump, thump' from the clouds raised him from his reverie. The cows kicked up their heels and hurried a little faster into the field, startled by the intrusion. George lifted his eyes to watch the helicopter's progress, and saw it pause in its flight and hover above the stone before turning east and heading on its way. I wonder if they spotted anything, thought George, maybe they did and maybe they didn't, but, hopefully, he would be able to start the process of the world noticing something that night in the pub.

As he entered the Crown George saw that David and Jonathan were already in residence at the bar. These two had certainly made an impact during their short stay; their brand of wit and the stories they told were well liked by all the regulars, and it seemed that some of them were becoming even more frequent visitors to the pub since these two had taken up their roles as the pub wags.

"Hi Lad, how are you? Can I get you another of those to keep the first company?" George asked, tapping him on the shoulder.

"That would be grand. If you don't mind," Lad answered.

"George wandered over to the bar, "Hello chaps. How goes it?" he asked.

"Fine," they replied.

"Well that is if you don't count the eighty bruises that I received today." Jonathan grumbled. "You see," he said turning to the interested group around him, "I've become a test pilot for motorized baked bean cans."

"He is referring to the fact," David explained, "that today he rode my highly prized Norton motorbike."

"Motorbikes have brakes."

"It has brakes."

"Wrong. It has one brake and very effective it is too—you stop dead when you hit it," Jonathan paused significantly, holding his audience. "It's called 'a Wall'."

"Just to put things into perspective," David said. "I will admit that the brakes were a little slack, but he was only going at about five miles an hour when he fell off."

"I didn't fall, that was a tactical move."

"If that was a tactical move then the Pope hates balconies."

Jonathan was about to respond, but the laughter from the group cut him off.

"Well," said George, "I don't know if the Pope likes balconies or not, but if you do want to get better acquainted with a wall, I can certainly help you out in that department."

"What do you mean?" Jonathan asked.

"You know you were saying you'd like to know about dry stone walling?" Well I've got a wall that needs repairing and I think I can spare you some time to show you how it's done."

"Ha," laughed Barney. "Trust George to try and get hold of some slave labour."

"Oh no, it isn't like that at all," George replied. "It will be an educational lecture."

"Oh so you're going to get them to pay for it then, are you?" Barney smiled.

"Well I don't mind. I'm game," said Jonathan. "David probably knows about it already, but I'll definitely give it a go. You never know, if I get good at it I could build my own wall and exhibit it at the Tate gallery as a piece of contemporary sculpture. I could earn a fortune."

"Oh well, I might have to ask for some money from you then," George winked. "Nicking my ideas. What's that, infringement of copy right?"

"Yes, something like that," Jonathan smiled. "Anyway, when do you want me to come to the farm?"

"Five thirty in the morning."

"What!"

"Only joking. About ten O' clock suit you?"

"That's fine. Just enough time to digest Mrs Pengelly's breakfast. In fact, I could bring some of her bread up. We could use it in the wall. It would last for centuries then."

In another pub, in another part of Cornwall, near the Culdrose air base, a man was sitting against the wall listening very intently to an airman's conversation at the next table. It wasn't difficult to eavesdrop as the airman concerned was becoming louder and more irate in his protestations the more his friends refused to take his story seriously.

"I'm telling you," the airman said, in a thick Scandinavian accent, "that stone has moved. I should know, I fly over it almost every day. First there were two stones, then there was one, and now that one has moved."

"Stones just don't move by themselves," his friends said.

"I'm not saying it has," the airman snapped. "It just looks like it has," he added more quietly."

The man in the corner slipped quietly from behind his table, gathered his brown raincoat from the seat, and left the pub.

George was in his field when he saw David's car entering his yard, and he turned to wave them over as the two men emerged into the chill air.

"Hi there," Jonathan said.

"Hello. Glad you could both make it." George replied, shaking them by the hand. "Many hands make light work eh? Do you know anything about dry stone walling then?" he asked David.

"A bit," he replied, "but there are lots of different methods aren't there and I'm always willing to learn something new."

"I'm glad to hear that, and yes, you're right, there almost as many ways of building a wall as there are of knocking one down. Except that some ways are better than others. Anyway, this is the wall that needs mending." he said, leading them over to a V-shaped gap in the west wall. "It shouldn't take long, but, we will need to partly to dismantle it before we can build it up again. We're also going to need a few more stones, nice flat ones like these. There should be some over by the stream. Do you think you could go and get me some, while I start to dismantle the wall? About this size should do," he said holding up a stone about six inches in length and two inches in width.

"Sure," said Jonathan. "I'll do it," and he strolled over towards the river.

George settled down to explain to David how the size of the stone selection was crucial to the strength of the wall, and was beginning to clear the rubble, when Jonathan came hurrying back towards them. "What's happened to the stone?" he asked. "Did you move it?"

"What stone?" George asked.

"The standing stone on the other side of the river." Jonathan replied. "It's moved."

"Oh rubbish," George said.

"Come on then, if you don't believe me. Come and see for yourselves."

David and George followed him over to the stone and looked at the trail it had made with bewilderment.

"I don't know what's happened," George said. "I certainly didn't move it. Someone should be told about this—the police or the press or something. Nobody's going to start moving things around on my land without my permission."

"The press already knows sir."

They turned around to see a man, with a brown raincoat over his arm coming towards them.

"Michael Thornton, Cornish Record," the man said, holding out his hand.

"Hello. Pleased to meet you," the others greeted in turn.

"You say your stone has been moved. Do you mind if I have a look?" the man asked.

"No certainly, go ahead," George replied.

The reporter moved carefully round the side of the stone. "It looks as though it's been pushed or pulled right through the ground," he said. "You can see where it's pushed the earth out of the way."

"You'd think it would have fallen over," George said.

"Yes you would, wouldn't you? But why would anyone want to move your rock?"

"Maybe they didn't," said David in his best Vincent Price voice. "Maybe it's just moving by itself, to fill the gap left in the stone circle." He smiled the smile of the criminally insane.

"What stone circle?" asked the reporter. "I can't see any circle."

"Ah. You have to know where to look," said David continuing his horror movie tone. "Those stones have been hidden for centuries. The circle has been broken. Now it must be restored. Ah Ha."

George glanced over at the reporter who was regarding David with some bewilderment, personally George felt like hugging the young man.

"It's true," George said. "There is a ring of small stones in the field. But I sold the large one that was in line with this, a couple of weeks ago."

"Do you think you could show me this stone ring?" the reporter asked.

"Sure. It's just over here."

The reporter studied the circle of stones carefully, and then looked over towards the stone that had moved. "Look," he said. "Would you mind if I brought someone along to take some pictures of this?"

"No, but you'd best be quick about it because I won't have this piece of land for much longer."

"Really? Why?" the reporter asked.

"Because the council want to take it away from me to build a new road."

"Do they now? Well don't go near the stone just yet. I'll be back as soon as I can."

They watched the reporter hurrying back to his car.

"Well," George said to Jonathan and David. "That's a bit rum isn't it? It looks as though we're going to be in the news. Shall we go back to our wall?" He put a hand on each of their shoulders and pushed them ahead. He did not want them to see him smiling, which was all he could do. He really felt like singing.

Niagara

Richly coloured light threw the distorted stained glass form of a peacock across the dark warmth of the oak breakfast table and onto the cold white marbled floor.

Two women sat at either end of the table and between them stretched a generation and an understanding of the need for silence. It was Celia Stanton, Marian's mother, who finally broke it.

"You should try and eat more."

"I don't feel like it."

"Well at least allow me to clear up."

"I'm not an invalid you know," Marian replied.

"Oh no? Then why are you limping?"

Marian smiled. "Well not much of an invalid anyway. I've got to keep busy or I just keep thinking about John, and I can't do that without feeling sad. Even if I think about the happy times we had together, all I can do is cry, because I know we won't be able to share anymore."

"I know, love," her mother said, "but you can't try and do too much. Just be sensible."

"When was I ever that? Even when I married John, you, Daddy and everybody else thought it was a bad decision. You just thought he was a no hope artist, full of grand impractical ideas which would never make him a living."

"Well we were wrong weren't we?"

"Yes, but even I didn't know that at the time. I thought the same as you really. I just knew he could see into me more deeply and express my feelings better than anyone else, even myself. It turned out that he could also express other people's feelings through his art, and he made a lot of money, but that really didn't matter to me. He just made me happy by being him, and I knew no one else could ever do the same."

Rising to comfort her daughter Mrs Stanton felt her own stab of pain when she saw her daughter, as unremitting as ever, immediately stifle her tears and turn from her with the bluff of rinsing off the plates.

Crash!

The force of the water that poured from the tap defied belief. A spoon flipped from the sink and hit the window, a dish, struck by the water, slammed against the corner of the stainless steel bowl and stayed there;

forcing the torrent back into the air to batter the ceiling with unrelenting fury. Marian screamed as the water cascaded down upon her.

Curtains, windows, floor, shelves, table, all were being drenched.

In bewilderment, Mrs Stanton watched as her daughter stepped backwards, slipped on the wet tiles and crashed to the floor, pulling the drying rack, full of plates down on top of her. It could not be happening, she lunged forward through the torrent, gasping as the stinging jet bit into her face, and struggled to stem the flow. The tap gave.

There was a stunned silence, broken only by the drip of water.

Mrs Stanton looked down on the prostrate form of her daughter, covered in white dinner plates, broken crockery and cutlery. The pile moved.

"Are you alright?"

"I think so," Marian said cautiously, taking her mother's hand to rise to her feet.

Mrs Stanton took in her daughter's bedraggled appearance, from the pieces of china sticking in her hair to the sopping dress. "You look awful," she commented.

"You don't look much better," Marian smiled. "In fact you look ridiculous," she laughed.

The laughter was infectious, and, as Marian came to her and hugged her, her mother realized that it was the first laugh she had heard her daughter utter in the five days since John had walked out of the door.

"Well, what do you think caused that?" Marian asked separating herself and her cloying clothes from her mother.

"I don't know," Mrs Stanton replied, wiping a tear from her eye, "But if we don't change out of these clothes soon we're going to catch our death." She bit her lip at the realisation of what she had just said.

"It's alright mum," Marian said placing her arm around her, "we can't avoid saying perfectly normal words just because of what I'm going through. It only emphasises them more if you do."

"I suppose you're right," her mother said. "But you can never be sure how sensitive people are. I think some people just avoid you in case they say the wrong thing. At least that's what I noticed when your father died."

"I know. I met Christine in the supermarket, she knew John had died, but she didn't mention it. I'm sure it was because she didn't want to intrude, but it just made me feel as though my feelings or John meant nothing to her. And I know that they do because we've been friends for so long."

"I know love, but where I come from we had a phrase, 'there's nowt so strange as folk', and, to be honest, there's no use getting philosophical about it either—especially when we're dripping wet. Come on let's go upstairs and get changed."

Mrs Stanton led her daughter by the hand and out into the hallway, but as they were walking past the entrance to John's studio, a strange intrusive scent caught her attention. It was at once both the fresh scent of wind-blown grass and the dank noisome odour of rotting leaves, but its most perturbing aspect was that it was one of those scents that spoke to her and said, 'remember'. However, there was no distinct memory and, try as she might; she could not recall when she had experienced the scent. She stopped outside the door. "You know," she said, "there's a funny smell coming from in there. Do you know what it is?"

"No," Marian replied, "I haven't noticed anything, but then I haven't liked going in there ever since the accident. John's stone is in there. I'll have to try and decide what to do with it, but he was so in love with the thing that I don't really want to get rid of it."

"Oh well, never mind. It's just that, I suppose, it smells a bit damp. But then aren't we all?" she said, laughing as she started up the stairs for her guest room.

Slipping off her soaking wet dress, she took it into the en suite bathroom and hung it over the shower rail.

Turning back she was about to rinse her dress through in the hand basin, when she noticed that the toilet had not stopped filling.

Cautiously lifting the top off the cistern, she placed it on the toilet seat and looked inside. Nothing appeared to be obviously wrong apart from the fact that the water was still running into the cistern and out of the overflow. Popping the ballcock under the water she watched it bob back to the surface; the flow of water seemed undiminished.

"Marian," she called.

Bang!

The top of the valve, running into the cistern, flew past her turned head and struck the ceiling.

"Marian!" she screamed, as the heavy brass valve thudded onto the floor beside her. "Help!"

The entire contents of the nearby reservoir seemed intent upon pouring into the bathroom. Forcing her hands over the water spout, she pushed with all her weight, fanning out the column into a mushroom, which effectively doused every square inch of the bathroom with water.

"What are you doing?" Marian called from the doorway.

So taken aback was she, by the totally inane nature of this remark that Mrs Stanton temporarily relinquished her hold on the pipe, allowing the jet of water to once more play across the ceiling. "I'm trying to stop this water coming out," she cried. "Now find the stopcock and turn it off."

"But I don't know where it is."

"Well find it. It should be under the sink in the kitchen."

Pushing all her weight once more onto the water outlet, whilst Marian hurried downstairs, Mrs Stanton waited for the water to subside—but it didn't.

"What are you doing?" she shouted downstairs.

"My flower bulbs are under here, I've got to be careful with them."

"Sod the bulbs," she swore, as the water was lifting her hair and slip. "Find the blasted tap and turn it off."

"I'm doing the best I can."

"Well do better!"

More might have been said, but each time Mrs Stanton tried to open her mouth it was filled, at very high pressure, by the cold water. She was seriously considering having another attempt at saying something when the flow stopped. She collapsed over the basin gasping for breath.

She heard footsteps on the stairs.

"Are you alright?" Marian asked.

"Yes," she gasped, "but the room isn't."

It was true: the place was indeed a mess; water was dripping from everywhere, the towels were lying in a pool of water, the louvered doors to the airing cupboard were allowing small streams of water to run out, and the once opaque curtains, sticking to the dripping window pane, were now so wet that they were translucent.

"I think I need a drink," Marian said.

"What you need is a plumber," Mrs Stanton replied.

Earthquake

The Bunch of Grapes was a service man's pub, and just as The Crown had its own character so did this. However, whereas the Crown drew its patrons together under its familiar intimacy, the 'Grapes' purpose built and cavernous interior, begged its patrons to spread out and fill its sterile vacuum.

Like a verbal football match, ribald shouts were flung and passed across the bar from one scattered group to another, as copious quantities of beer and spirits were bought and consumed. However, when the door opened, even amongst this cacophonous mayhem, no one failed to notice the woman who entered.

Clad in a figure hugging dark green suit, the woman strode into the public house with a confidence, which might wrongly suggest that she were a regular customer. She stopped centre stage, scanned her surroundings, and made her way to where a bulky man sat dwarfing the screwed down table in front of him.

"Lieutenant Hákon isn't it?" Her question was issued into an almost silent environment.

The man's gaze moved from his glass, across the floor and up his inquisitor's legs. It was a long journey, prolonged by the fact that the woman was displaying her assets to the best advantage.

"Yes," the man replied.

"My name is Jane Appleby from the Daily Herald, but you can call me Jane."

"Snorri," the man said.

"I said I'm Jane Appleby," the woman started.

"No my Christian name is Snorri. You can call me Snorri."

"Oh. I'm sorry, I thought ..." she hesitated. "May we start again?"

"Certainly," the man said. "Can I get you a drink?"

"No. Let me get you one. What do you want?"

"I'll have another pint of lager thank you."

Snorri did not mind letting her go to the bar, it gave him a chance to watch those legs in action once more. They certainly strode with the assertiveness of someone who was used to being unhindered in her passage through life.

Snorri smiled as he saw the barman almost bound across to take her order, but, before she could be served, an airman slipped in beside her.

"Can I buy you a drink?" he heard the airman ask across the still quiet bar.

"No thank you."

"Why not? I'll buy those for you."

"Because I wouldn't want you to squander your money on a lost cause. And, if one of us has to waste their money, it should be me. I must earn a lot more than you."

"So you're going to buy me a drink?"

"No. I'm going to buy him a drink," she indicated Snorri. "And I do believe he out-ranks you."

Snorri smiled up at Jane as she returned to the table with the drinks.

"You certainly know how to handle men," Snorri said.

"Only those that come complete with a handle," she replied.

"Handle?"

"Never mind. I'm interested in your story about the stone. "

"I've already told that to a man from the Record."

"Yes, I know. But it wasn't reported in much detail, and I want to remedy that."

"What exactly do you want to know?"

"Everything: what you saw, what you thought, what you learnt."

"Do you want to interview me here?"

"Wherever is convenient."

"Then why don't we drive out there and I can describe exactly what happened."

"Hmm. Would it be possible for me bring a photographer along with us?"

"I don't see why not."

"Good. I'll arrange it then." She got up to find the phone and Snorri returned to his glass; a long red hair lay stretched across it, disrupting its creamy head. Smiling, he lifted it from the glass, wrapped it around his finger and raised it to his enquiring nose.

The next day Snorri was in a car with Jane and Peter Andrews, the photographer, on their way to the stones.

"You know it's scenery like this," Peter said as he drove, "that makes me want to give up journalism and go into landscape photography. Just look at it. There must be at least five hundred shades of green, fifty of brown, God knows how many yellows, and look, there are even shades of blue in the bushes, and what happens if I take a picture of it? It becomes a two inch, smudged, black and grey picture on poor quality paper that someone glances at and then throws away."

"It must be hard having the artist in you so disregarded by others," Jane said.

"It is."

"Well, who knows, if you keep on collecting a quality portfolio you could even end up working for Time, where your talents might be truly appreciated. In the meantime, I suggest you appreciate how lucky you are to be living with all this wonderful scenery around you. It might also be worth your while to consider how incredibly lucky you will be to still be alive if we go back to London without a nice set of photographs to accompany the story."

"Point taken M'Lady. I'll just drive then shall I?"

"What a good idea."

Snorri, sitting in the back of the car with Jane, felt a bit bemused by the turn of the conversation, and decided to change its course.

"Do you know what you should do to get some good photographs of the area?" he asked.

"No," replied Peter. "What?"

"Go up in a helicopter. You get to see a lot more that way."

"Now that is a good idea," Peter agreed. "Could you take me up then?"

"Certainly. Not in one of ours of course, but if you hired a private one I'm licensed to fly civilian aircraft."

"That would be excellent."

"Hang on a minute," Jane said. "Before you go getting your hopes up, I think you should know that the paper's budget for this article probably doesn't run to the hiring of helicopters. So we will just have to do as well as we can on the little that we have.

"Mind you," she continued slyly, "you never know, if we can make this into a big enough story our budget might just change."

George heard the car draw up outside and peered through the kitchen window. It was probably the reporter who had rung him yesterday. This could make his story national news. He reminded himself not to appear too eager for their attentions—he did not want them to suspect his motives.

As George watched, he saw the car door open and a long pair of stockinged legs emerge. He had grasped the doorknob before he managed to catch hold of himself. Wait, he reminded himself as he hid behind the door, wait until she knocks.

The sharp rap announced her arrival. George counted slowly to thirty and opened the door: "Hello," he said.

"Hello Mr Penton, I'm Jane Appleby. I spoke to you on the phone yesterday."

"Ah yes. You're the reporter aren't you?"

"Yes that's right: from Today."

"And you want to look at my stones?"

"As well as interview you, if that would be possible."

"Oh it's possible alright; just a little inconvenient that's all.

"There are so many people wanting to talk to me and to look at my stones that I hardly have a chance to get on with any work."

"But if you speak to us, Mr Penton, you will get nation-wide publicity, and that can't be bad for you."

"Oh it can't, can't it? Well what about when all those people start traipsing over my field. They'll ruin it they will. I'll have to start charging admission."

"In that case you might make some money out of it. As well as extending your reputation: not only will you be famous in the village, you'll be the most talked about man in the country."

"And just what have you heard about my reputation?"

"I've heard that you're a bit of a lad Mr Penton."

"Oh have you? And have you heard anything else?"

"They also say that you're a bit of a ladies' man. And let's just say that I can quite easily see how they might arrive at that conclusion."

"Really? Well I suppose that I'd best take you to see the stones then."

"Before you do I'd just like to introduce you to some friends of mine," she turned and indicated her companions who were unloading the car.

George greeted them in turn, but it was with some surprise that he felt Jane Appleby slip her arm through his: "Shall we go to the stones then, before they start coming to us?" she smiled.

George allowed himself to be led away, happy in the knowledge that his act of reluctant acquiescence to the media's demands was beginning to pay dividends. For one, this gorgeous reporter was obviously trying to pacify him with her flirtations, and that was fine by him.

"Ah," Jane said, "I see you have some men working on your wall. Hi chaps. Nothing like a bit of honest toil in the sunshine eh?"

"Chaps?" David said turning round. "That's a bit informal isn't it? Do we know you?"

"Err, Jane Appleby, this is David Pengelly and Jonathan Moseley," George introduced with some embarrassment. "They're learning all about dry stone walling."

"So George is teaching you all the tricks of the trade is he?" Jane asked.

"Yes it's the open university," David said.

"Really?" I didn't know that you had university lecturer listed amongst your many talents George."

"He doesn't. It's the Open Air University," David responded.

"Oh I see, a little joke. Well shall we go through to look at this stone?" she linked her arm through George's once more and towed him away, but as the quartet took their leave, George heard David's voice float to him across the field: "Patronizing cow."

George led them across the small bridge he had made to the other side of the river and followed the river downstream towards the stone.

"Do you have any ideas how the stone may have moved?" Jane asked, striding along easily beside him.

"Not really," George said. "I only know that it has moved. Some people think that it might have been moving to fill in the gap left in the stone circle."

Jane wandered closer to the stone and brushed it with her hand, "But that's not really plausible is it?" she said, "And there is no way of proving it is there?"

"There are ways of tracing the movements of an object," David called, from the other side of the river, "but that usually involves studying its tracks. And as you are walking all over the area that will make the process rather difficult."

"Oh," Jane jumped back as though she had suddenly found herself standing on hot coals. "That was stupid of me wasn't it? I didn't think. I do apologize.

"Have you got your pictures yet?" she asked, turning to Peter.

"Yes I'm just about done," he replied.

"Okay well let's go back, carefully. We'll get some pictures of the stone circle and finish off the interview."

"I am truly sorry," Jane told David, as she returned over the bridge.

"Never mind," David said, proffering a helping hand, "we all make mistakes."

George was the last to come across and, as he did so, he looked at the riverbank. Something about it was not quite right, but he did not know what.

Strange Phenomena

"I don't really know what to say," the plumber said as he brought his head out from under the sink. "All the seals on your taps are in perfectly good working order. It's just that the pressure in the pipes is huge."

"What could cause that?" Marian asked.

"There's actually not many things that can cause such a sudden increase in pressure. I only know of one similar occasion. One of the water companies introduced brand new pumping stations, just before they became privatised. The problem was that their customers' old pipes weren't able to cope with the extra pressure and started to crack."

"So could it be a similar thing here?"

"No, not really. The water supply is the same as it always was, and none of your neighbours are affected. I am afraid that it is just high pressure running up to your house. It's as though you were sitting at the bottom of a very deep well. It could be air somewhere in your pipes, but that should have run off by now."

"Isn't that's a bit odd?"

"Yes, it is."

"Well isn't there anything you can do about it?"

"Not really. In theory, I can slightly close down the valve in the mains supply to the house. It is on your land. But then that would only cause an increase in the pressure in the mains pipe, which could damage it—if it's not damaged already."

"So what you are saying is that we have to be prepared to live with a geyser erupting in our sink every time we turn on the tap."

"Yes, for the moment. You could try running more water off in case there is some air in the centre, but what I suggest you do is write to the local water authority and to your council and explain the situation."

"And then they'll just write back and tell me to get a plumber."

The plumber sighed:

"Not if I give you an accompanying letter that explains the situation from my point of view."

The door to the kitchen swung open, and Marian's mother stood in the doorway, dripping wet.

"You turned the water back on didn't you?" she said.

"Err, yes," the plumber said.

"I guessed. I'm beginning to get a washer woman's body as well as hands."

The others watched in silence as, with as much dignity as she could muster, she turned and squelched back up the hallway.

Letting the plumber out of the door, Marian was surprised to see a black and white border collie sitting in the middle of her drive. One forepaw held up and quivering, it was staring expectantly over its shoulder. Following its gaze, Marian saw a cloth capped old man standing ramrod straight at the end of her drive, seemingly studying the house.

"I'll send that letter along with the invoice then," the plumber said going to his van.

"What? Oh yes, thank you." She turned her attention back to the drive, but, although she was in time to see the dog trotting back down the path, the old man had gone.

Teatime Talks

Jonathan was paying for his excesses of the previous evening. After ten pints of the local brew, he felt like a new man—Frankenstein's monster to be precise. A man with poor limb co-ordination, a tongue transplanted from an elephant and a head that had recently had 10,000 volts warped through it. He sat slumped over a mug of coffee on the kitchen table, cradling his head—partly to take its weight and partly to avoid the sight of young Danny Jones tucking into the dish of ice-cream that Mrs Pengelly had set in front of him.

David came through with the morning paper in his hand. "Ah, Danny my boy. Guess what?" he said.

"The pipes, the pipes are calling?" Jonathan hazarded.

"No, not quite," David said with a smile."But the attention of the country has indeed been called to focus on our locality."

"What is that meant to mean?" asked his mother.

"That, 'mater', means that the story of George Penton's moving stone has been printed in the national press, but, that is not all. A group of experts are coming to look at the stones, and, to quote the paper, 'Study this hitherto unknown circle of stones, which have propelled themselves into the public eye'."

"I don't see what all the fuss is about," said Danny.

"No, neither do I," said David. "It's just that you don't often hear of moving stones."

"Well it only moved a few feet," Danny said. "I won the sprint race and the long jump for my year on sports day, but I didn't get a mention in the paper."

Jonathan chuckled. "Yes," he said, "but you're not over two thousand years old. If you can still move a few feet when you're that old, maybe they'll report that in the paper too."

Mrs Pengelly brought over a large carrier bag and placed it on the table in front of Danny:

"There you are Danny," she said. "That's the curtain. Tell your mother that the tear is in the lining at the top. And let her know that she will be doing me a great favour if she can repair it."

"Okay, Mrs Pengelly," Danny said, getting up and carrying the bag to the door. "Goodbye. Thanks for the ice cream."

"That's alright. Goodbye and do thank your mother."

The door closed.

"Nice kid," said David.

"Yes, and quite wise for a twelve year old," Mrs Pengelly said. "I mean here we are, about to be descended on by reporters, so called experts and who knows who else; and for what? An old stone. It's mad."

"Mad it may be, but you're likely to do quite well out of it," said Jonathan.

"How might that be?"

"The people who come to look at the stone are going to want somewhere to stay. As you're not far away they might well stop with you, especially if you do the right sort of advertising."

"What sort of advertising?"

"I don't know. David and I could stand by the stone and sell some of those delicious rock cakes you made and wrap a map around them to tell people where you are."

"I haven't made any rock cakes."

"What were those hard little cakes we had yesterday then?"

"Fruit scones."

"Oh."

Danny walked away from the guesthouse, head down, mind racing with injured pride. Last Saturday he had competed in his school's sports day and beaten Billy Carmichael, who everyone had thought was bound to win. He had trained by running all the way through his paper round every day, and his mother had said that if he won he might even get his name in the local paper, but had he? No. All they seemed to care about was a moving stone. Well, if that could become famous why couldn't he?

He threw the bag over his shoulder and ran home. Arriving, out of breath, he flung the door open and hurried into the living room where he dropped the bag and headed for the coffee table.

"Did you get a paper mum?" he asked.

"Excuse me," his mother said, "but could you tell me where you left your manners? You don't just come charging in here without saying hello, and then expect me to answer your shouts do you?"

"I'm sorry mum. That's Mrs Pengelly's curtain, and she said to thank you very much."

"That's better," his mother said, "and thank you for going for me.

"The paper's in the kitchen."

Danny went through and started looking through The Cornishman. The story on the stones was much as David had read it, but, although it mentioned that experts would be arriving, it did not say when that would be. In theory then they could arrive tomorrow, and in that case, he did not have much time to act; he would have to do it tonight.

The cupboard under the stairs held the sharp lemon tang of furniture polish, the heavy wax pungency of shoe polish and a multitude of odds, ends and gadgets. Danny burrowed down into the clutter and finally emerged victorious. It was still there. He looked down at the can of red car spray paint in his hand. Soon his name would be known throughout the country.

Objective Attained

The stone-flagged floor of the kitchen was excellent for keeping the room cool in summer but, during the winter, it could suck the heat from exposed feet in a matter of minutes. So, it was with stockinged feet on the scrubbed and pristine table, that George leant back in his chair and contemplated his predicament. The press were beginning to ask the wrong questions, or, more accurately, the wrong question: what was the identity of the person who had bought his stone?

George considered his options. Telling the press that it was John Dally who had purchased the stone might result in the poor, seemingly decent, man becoming embroiled in a lot of unnecessary investigations, but, not least, it might conclude with public pressure forcing him to give the money back to the sculptor for the return of the stone.

If, however, he continued to try and fob the press off with saying that he was unable to reveal the buyer's name on the grounds of customer confidentiality, it had several advantages: he would keep his money, he would appear to be an honourable man and it would enhance the mystery surrounding the stone. His one fear was that if the press suspected that he were stalling they might also be wary of his motives. Still, why shouldn't he have his own little mystery surrounding him?

Coming back down to earth, George straightened his chair and went to the fridge for a beer. Not unusually, the door had stuck, but, as with much else in the temporal world, it yielded to his pressure and flew open. It was unfortunate that it met his leg along the way and struck up an acquaintance with his kneecap.

Limping back to his chair, George carried four bottles; one to place against the long red weal on his leg, and three to help him sleep.

The rain continued its drizzle and softened the mud around the crouching figure in the field. At last, the solitary light from the Penton farm was extinguished, and the telltale beam through the window ceased to disturb the field's black ambiguity. Danny rose to his feet, sodden and cold, but determined. He was not going to turn back now. One and a half hours of waiting in the pouring rain had not only strengthened his resolve but it had also given him time to think. No longer would he simply daub his name across the stone—that would merely lead the police directly to him. He needed a sign: something like the mark of Zorro, which everyone would recognize. His initials seemed a safe bet; they would make him chief suspect, and he would be talked about, but they would not prove his guilt.

Danny crept slowly around the edge of the field and over the crude plank bridge that had been set across the river. A dark treacherous grease lay across its surface—a combination of the mud from the shoes of the stone's previous visitors and the incessant rain. However, Danny was twelve years old—as nimble as a mountain goat and as confident in his immortality as a newly hatched chick oblivious to the shadow of the circling hawk. He crossed the bridge without breaking stride or pausing for thought.

A cold stinging squall slapped across his face as he set foot on the bank. He tried to pull the hood further over his head, but it was stretched to capacity. The stone should give some shelter. He ran towards it, bent double, but risked a glance towards his goal. Suddenly and brilliantly, a cold white light illuminated the stone. He flung himself to the ground and rolled into the shadows, desperately seeking the light's source.

It was the moon. The warm cloudy skies had opened a gap in their cover to channel the light from the bright orb down onto the stone. However, even as Danny watched the thick clouds modestly covered the exposed sky and darkness regained control.

With a gasp of relief, Danny levered himself from the mud, and shivering from the cold slime clutching his clothes to his body, hurried on to his appointment with the stone.

There it was. The menhir reared out of the darkness and towered above its diminutive, would-be, assailant. Standing at the end of the channel carved by George Penton, and fed by a rich network of arteries, the stone was surrounded by a dark pool of mud laden rain water that overflowed in one turgid vein to the river, but, between the rivulets, there was mud, and rising haphazardly from the mud there were tufts of grass—stepping stones.

With balletic movements, Danny moved from one dark grey island to the next. Arms outstretched he resembled a tightrope walker, except that it was no balancing pole clutched between his hands, just an old can of spray paint.

One hand on the stone for support he pulled the top off the can with his teeth and leant over the pool to complete his deed, but one of his feet slipped in the mud, he half recovered, slipped again and fell—chest slamming into the stone. The stone rocked forward, the can fell from his grip below the stone, he tumbled into the muddy channel and the stone rocked back.

There was an explosion.

Jacket still unbuttoned from the rush to leave the house, George felt the beer erupt back into his mouth at the sight of crimson horror before him. For there, revealed in the torch beam, was a blood filled pool and the shattered fragments of a leg trapped by the stone against the bank, but, worst of all, was the pale innocent face, upturned above the red stained water—an angel baptized in blood.

New Faces

George glanced at his watch. Nine o'clock on the dot, at least the man was punctual.

The two small vans stopped in front of him and George could not help but feel nervous as he waited for the entrance of he who could be the chief witness for his prosecution. He took a deep breath and steadied himself as the door of the leading vehicle opened and a tall rigid man emerged. With straight raven black hair swept back from the brow and high cheekbones the man cut an imposing figure, and he walked with the purpose of one obeying an order, an order that told him to make straight for George.

"Good morning," the man called. "Mr Penton isn't it? I am Alexander Balchin. We spoke yesterday."

"Yes. Good morning." George was relieved that his body did not accompany the movement when he shook hands. He stepped back. "Although I'm afraid I didn't take in everything you said over the phone. Could you tell me again who it is you're working for?"

"Indeed I can." Balchin replied. "As I said earlier, Mr Penton, we are connected with the Nature Conservancy Council, and it is they who may, on the basis of our findings, designate your stones an ancient monument and your field an S.S.S.I. That is to say," he quickly continued, "a Site of Special Scientific Interest."

However, George was not really listening; he was too absorbed by the sight of the man before him who, eyes closed, hands behind his back, was weaving his torso to and fro in gentle gyratory emphasis to his words. George found it almost impossible to dispel the comic image of a large black crow pecking the ground.

"They are types of conservation order," the man explained. "You may even receive a grant in return for your help in maintaining the site, but, as I say, that all rather depends on the findings of our investigation."

The gyrations ceased abruptly. "I trust that the police have finished with their examination of the area?" There was a new focus and sharpness in Balchin's words and posture—as if for the first time he valued George's opinion.

"Um," George faltered, unnerved by the sudden eye contact, "yes."

"Good. I hope there wasn't too much damage?"

"Well he did lose a lot of blood, and his leg was quite badly injured, but they think he's going to be alright."

"I was actually enquiring about the stone, Mr Penton. Although, of course, I am pleased to hear that the boy is getting better; but the heavens know how much he may have set back our investigations." Balchin turned back to his companions. "Ah I see the equipment is unloaded. Would you be so kind as to escort us to your stone circle, Mr Penton?"

Mr Penton? Would he ever wish to be on first name terms with this man? George suspected not.

Snatching up two large bags, Balchin overtook George's lead to stride confidently ahead into the field, leaving the others to struggle with the remaining equipment in his wake.

"I suppose I had better introduce you to the rest of the team, Mr Penton," Balchin called over his shoulder. "Our engineer, who will be trying to find out how and why your stone moved, is John Laine. All our measurements and notes are made by Mark Andrews, and our photography expert is Matthew Reece." George turned to see a good-humoured grin break over the ruddy features of the large man hurrying up behind them with a tripod over his shoulder.

"It's a pity your name's not Luke, Mr Balchin," George commented. "Then we could have had all four gospels represented."

"I'm no evangelist or saint, Mr Penton."

"No," was all George could think to say. He filled the silence: "What are you actually going to be looking for?"

"Mainly we will be trying to estimate the age of the circle. To see if it was built in the same period as the other circles or if it is just a modern folly."

"And how do you intend to do that?"

"We have our ways Mr Penton, we have our ways."

George decided not to press the matter, but merely called the party to a halt when they reached the depression where John Dally's stone had once stood. He stepped to one side and watched with interest as Balchin withdrew a compass from his pocket and, head bowed over the small dial, slowly circled the site.

"It seems we have some good news," the archaeologist said, becoming erect as he slipped the compass back into his pocket. "The stone which stood here lay West South West to the rest of the circle, as indeed does its companion across the river, the one that supposedly moved."

"What does that prove?" George asked.

"Nothing in itself, Mr Penton. It is just that many of the circles in Cornwall have their largest stone lying in that direction to the circle. Or, in the case of Boscawen-un, that is where its quartz stone lies.

The major anomaly here is that the stones which comprise the other circles aren't usually as small as these."

"Perhaps this circle is more recent than the others," George speculated.

"Why do you say that?"

"Because as technology advances it often becomes miniaturized."

Balchin smiled. "Let's hope it's not too modern, Mr Penton.

Eruption From The Id

Grey tiles covered the floor and emerged along the central isle and between the twin regimented lines of white and grey beds, cloaked with stiff white linen, and, whilst the wood of the bedside cabinet might have seemed out of character with its hard cold surroundings, it was obviously laminated. However, the stand was in total keeping with the room; once white its paint had faded to cream and had chipped off in several places to reveal cold clean metal beneath. Rising from the stand, on its tripod of legs, was a second telescopic section of gleaming chrome, which held the bag; the bag that slowly dripped its contents into the regulating tube, past the comforting hand of the mother and into the arm of her son.

Mrs Jones pulled her plastic chair closer to Danny's bed and held his hand as she watched the clear drip slowly emptying life into his veins.

"He's still asleep I see."

Mrs Jones looked up towards the blonde haired doctor, standing at the foot of the bed. "Yes," Mrs Jones replied, "I only hope it's doing him some good."

"I'm sure it is," the doctor smiled. "He's had quite a shock and he'll need a lot of rest to get over it.

"My name's Ann O'Brien, by the way. I am the Senior Registrar who will be looking after Danny. Have you any questions that you would like to ask me?"

"Only the one really: how is he?"

The doctor came around the side of the bed and, smoothing her white coat beneath her, took a seat on the bed next to Danny's arm.

"As you know," she started, "Danny lost a lot of blood, but we have given him a transfusion and that shouldn't be a problem anymore. He is also sleeping rather a lot, and when he is awake he doesn't want to eat. It's because of this and because he is slightly dehydrated that he is on the drip; but he should soon be off that. There is a rather large bump on the back of his head, but all our tests suggest that there is no brain damage. Apart from that, he has some severe bruising on his wrists; we're not quite sure how he received those. Then, of course, there are his leg injuries; his right leg was severely damaged. Our surgeons have pieced it together as best they can, and once he is slightly better he will be going to see the physiotherapists, but I fear he will always walk with a slight limp."

"Will he be able to run? He did love to run."

"To be honest I don't think he will win any races, but, you never know, there is always hope.

"I'm afraid I am going to have to go now, but if ever you want to talk to me about anything at all, just phone the hospital and ask the switchboard to bleep me." she patted Mrs Jones' hand, and got up to leave.

"Thank you," Danny's mother said.

"Think nothing of it. Bye."

Mrs Jones smiled as she watched Ann O'Brien take her leave. It was good to have support and Danny was obviously in good hands. Fondly looking down upon her son, she saw that his lips were moving, almost imperceptibly, but rhythmically, as if he were whispering a mantra. She bent closer, trying to catch the words, and captured instead the sickening sweet stench of her son's breath, as foetid as the cold vapours which tell of a carcass in a cave, but she held her ground.

"It's dark," Danny whispered. "I can't see it."

"What can't you see, love?" she asked softly, stroking the glass chill of his brow.

Danny was gasping for air: "It's cold, I can't see, can't breathe," his chest was heaving, trying to drag air into his lungs.

"Doctor!" his mother called.

"It doesn't want me," his chest heaved with the fight for air, "it's pushing me, pushing me out. Help me!" With a scream, Danny surged upwards with fierce energy sending his mother sprawling from the bed, the drip stand crashing to the ground and ripping the catheter from his arm to leave the sticking plaster waving like a banner over the trickle of blood that wound down through the fair hairs to splatter crimson across the tiles.

Struggling from beneath the stand, which had fallen across her, his mother desperately, tried to right the drip, "Help! Help me!" she cried.

A nurse sprang from behind the reception desk and rushed to her aid as Ann rushed through from the other ward and, with quick action, managed to stem the flow of blood from the arm. She settled the calm but still panting boy back onto his pillow.

Danny turned his head towards his mother, kneeling by the bedside, but the smile that he bestowed upon her was cold and empty and when he parted his lips to speak, it was no longer a whisper: "I'm out."

Source Finder

The afternoon soap opera was not very good, but it was addictive; and despite the fact that its cast argued and had affairs with monotonous regularity, it had become ritual viewing for Mrs Stanton. So, when the doorbell rang, she got up, but lingered in the television room, one finger resting as an umbilical cord on the sofa back, until she discovered whether the TV family's dog had pulled through its operation. Then and only then did she reluctantly leave to the accompaniment of the soap's theme tune.

She assumed that Marian must have forgotten her key, but a very different character greeted her when she opened the door. A tall elderly man swept off his cap and issued her with a neat courteous bow. "Good afternoon," he smiled. "Are you the lady of the house?

"Well I'm certainly one of them. How may I help you?"

"I believe that I may be the one to help you. I'm afraid I don't have a card, but allow me to introduce myself: Alfred Dart, and this here is Bess." A black and white collie wound itself out from behind his legs to sit by his side; her bright brown eyes pinned expectantly on her master. "I believe you have a water problem?"

She was taken aback. How did he know? "Yes, we do. Are you a plumber?"

"Not in the conventional sense, but then I don't believe that you have a conventional problem."

"That's an understatement. So, how do you think you can help us?"

"I'm afraid I haven't got a simple answer to that one. Would it be possible for me to come in and explain?"

"Oh, of course. Please do. I'm Celia Stanton by the way." A cautionary warning fluttered in the back of her mind. Should she be inviting a total stranger into the house? Maybe not, but here was a man whose genteel manners seemed of another age: an age when a lady need never fear a gentleman's cruelty. He stepped over the threshold and the dog quickly followed, nuzzling his hand. Could a cruel man win such obvious affection from an animal? She hoped not.

It had not been a good day for Marian: the haircut and the shopping for new clothes, whilst intended to cheer her up, had simply made her feel guilty at trying to cheat her grief. She decided that she did not really want to be happy, and the rain, broken shopping bags and bird droppings on her scarf had certainly helped towards that goal. Therefore, returning home to discover her mother sitting cosily at the kitchen table, with a dog at her feet and talking to the very man who had so disconcerted her a few days earlier, somehow made her day seem complete.

"Hello dear," her mother welcomed. "This is Mr Dart. He thinks he can help us with our water problem."

Mr Dart rose to greet her: "Good afternoon Mrs Dally."

"How do you do Mr Dart," Marian said, slipping off her coat. "And how do you think you can help us?"

"Mr Dart's a dowser, dear." Marian's mother answered for him. "He finds water with his dowsing rod."

"That's not really our problem is it? We know where the water is. Every time we turn on our taps it's like Niagara Falls."

"But he could find out where it's all coming from," her mother persisted.

"I don't care where it's coming from, I just wish there weren't so much of it.

"I'm sorry if I appear rude, Mr Dart, but I regard dowsing as nothing short of Mumbo Jumbo, and I really can't see how you might help us."

"Marian!" her mother exclaimed.

"It's alright Mrs Stanton," Mr Dart said, holding up a placatory hand. "There are those who believe and those who do not. Those who don't are often converted, whilst those who do are never proved in error. I will leave you my number in case you change your mind." He looked up from the table where he was writing. "You have a very real problem here, Mrs Dally," he said, "and I don't think it's going to go away. Don't hesitate to call me if you change your mind. I'll show myself out. Come on Bess. Thank you for the tea, Mrs Stanton. Goodbye." He strode into the hallway, there was a click of the latch and he was gone.

"I did not bring you up to speak to people like that," Marian's mother remonstrated.

"I'm sorry, but I just didn't feel up to feigning belief in that nonsense."

Mrs Stanton glared at her daughter and snatched up the teapot from the table: "Get a cup, sit down and I'll tell you a story," she ordered.

The tone of voice denied argument and Marian was too tired to offer resistance. She obediently fetched a cup, slumped into the still warm chair, vacated by Mr Dart, and forlornly watched as her mother poured the tea and began her story: "In 1937 I was working in the Midlands as personal secretary for a large firm of mining surveyors, when our geologists thought that they had found a particularly rich coal seam in the Coventry area. This was highly important, as nearly all of our energy, both electricity and gas, came from coal, and, as there was the threat of war, we couldn't afford to rely on foreign imports.

All the tests we ran seemed to be encouraging and all that was needed as the final proof was to drill a test bore. For this, however, we needed a very large water supply, which would help to both power the equipment and wash out the slurry. It was going to be a very expensive operation; we had to pay for a special firm of engineers from Belgium to come in and do the actual boring and they had to use replaceable diamond crowns on the tip of the bore: diamonds being the only things that were hard enough to cut through the rock.

"Everything was ready, but our geologists couldn't find a local supply of water that was large enough to cater to our needs. We needed a supply of several thousand tons of water an hour. It looked like the whole project would have to be cancelled. That is until we called in an old dowser; he found the water we needed, the bore was sunk, and the mine went into operation.

"Now, that's a true story. So rather than being so scathing about Mr Dart's offer of help, I suggest you think again."

Theories Aired

Peter looked down and saw that there was still enough dew on the long grass to leave dark trails across the leather of his brown brogues and the beige cotton turn-ups of his trousers. Telling Jane to go on ahead, he lifted his camera to his eye, focussed on the group of men ahead, pulled back, opened the aperture by two stops and fired. He could already see the ambiguity of the finished picture: grey upright forms thrusting into the white glare of the sky—a silhouette of scientists or was it the circle of stones they studied? His editor, the philistine, would look at it and say, 'Too arty', and it would be cast aside, consigned to his portfolio—his treasure chest of personal achievement.

He slipped the cap back on the lens, and continued on his course across the field to catch up with Jane.

"Fine day isn't it?" George called as he approached. "Are you well?"

"Mustn't grumble Mr Penton," Peter answered.

"I don't know why not, everyone else seems to," George replied. "Do you think you're going to be able to get a picture of me in the paper this time?"

"I've no idea. I can take a picture if you want, but it's down to the picture editor as to what gets printed."

"Ah well, I may just have to wait for fame a little bit longer then." George smiled and continued. "You don't know everyone here do you? I'd best put that to rights straight away. Jane and Peter, this is Alexander Balchin, who is in charge of the operation, this here is Mark, the chap over there with the camera is Matt, and John is the fellow wading about in the river. David and Jonathan you already know."

Jane stepped forward "Hello Mr Balchin," Jane said, shaking his hand. "I know something of you already; your work is highly regarded." A modest smile curled Balchin's lip, but Jane did not know him well enough to be sure whether it was authentic. "Have you come to any conclusions yet?" she asked.

"Only that we are dealing with quite an unusual circle, Miss ..."

"Appleby," she helped. "So why is the circle unusual, Mr Balchin?"

"Its dimensions: the diameter of this circle is over one hundred meters, whereas others in this area vary between twenty and forty." In cruciform pose he indicated the span of the circle with lank outstretched arms. "This circle covers an area of over one and a half acres."

Nearly all the field in fact," George cut in. "It was my grandfather who enclosed the circle in the field. It's only two acres, but I allow the cows to come in and graze it every so often, so it more or less earns its keep."

"It does you and your family credit that, until recently, you preserved the site so well," Balchin said. "Because, as I mentioned, this is a very interesting circle. Not only is its area larger than most, but the stones which make it up are much smaller than is usual."

"Have you any ideas why it was built like that?" Jane asked.

"Not at the moment," Balchin replied, "but of course it would have been much easier to build a circle of small stones."

"Why aren't they all built with small stones then?" Jane asked.

"I have a theory, and it is only that mind you, so I wouldn't quote me, that the circles needed to be seen. By that, I mean that they needed to be seen from a distance, as they were used for meeting places: possibly for ritual purposes or for trading purposes. For example, at Camborne, quite near here, there was a stone-axe factory, and close by, on Wendron Down, there were two circles where several axes were found. It is thought that such axes might have been taken there to be traded. A market place, such as this, would need to be found easily, and the large stones would make the circles easy to see from a long way off."

"Then why wasn't this circle made as easy to spot?" Jane asked.

"Perhaps it didn't need to be. Many circles were made close to water, in valleys or in the middle of a large area of open land. All of which act as natural guidelines; simply follow the river, walk down the valley or look across the open land, and you will see the stones nearby. This circle lies very close to the river and even has two large guide stones on either side of it, so that the actual stones of the nearby circle don't have to be that large."

"They only needed a small erection then," Jonathan put in.

"No thank you, I've just had one," David rejoined.

Balchin looked at David with disgust. "I don't think it is wise to mock those things which you clearly fail to understand," he snapped.

"Mock. I Mock?" David said. "I'm no mocker, am I Jonathan?"

"Certainly not." Jonathan said, plucking at a stem of grass. "If he was a Mocha he would be brown and taste of coffee. And he doesn't."

"I can tell you that your sort wouldn't have been tolerated in those days; no matter what you tasted like," Balchin sneered.

"What days?" asked David, "The days when the circles were made? What do you know of our 'sort', and what the architects of this circle would have thought of us?"

"He was a member of the Order of Bards Ovates and Druids," Jane commented with an arch smile.

"How do you know that?" Balchin asked, his surprise barely overcoming his anger.

"I'm a Journalist," Jane replied simply.

"The Order of Bards Ovates and Druids," David said. "Isn't that a branch of the Ancient Order of Druids, inaugurated in 1781? Not, really, that ancient is it?"

"Our traditions go back much further. Before Christ in fact."

"I'm sure they do. As far as I am aware the Celtic priests, or Druids, arrived in Britain in about 500 BC, but by then even Stonehenge, which was one of the later circles, was 1000 years old. If your brethren used the henges at all, they merely took possession of what was already there; like so many Cuckoos.

"Come on, Jonathan; let's leave this latter day Cuckoo to his work." He turned to take his leave and collided with a figure who had appeared beside him. "Oh! Sorry" David apologized, "Michael Thornton, Cornish Record, isn't it?"

"It is indeed. Just off are you?"

"Yes, afraid so. We're going to grab something to eat and then go onto the Crown. Why don't you join us later?"

"I might just do that. Bye," Michael Thornton switched his attention toward Jane. "Hello Miss Appleby," he said. "Developed a taste for my story, have you?"

"It's an acquired taste."

"Just like some people."

"Are you referring to me?"

"Why would you think that? I was just making a general comment."

"I just sense that you're not happy with me. All I have done Mr Thornton, is to take your story to a larger audience, but, if you feel that I have trodden on your toes, I'm sorry. Would you be interested in having a drink with me in order to promote inter paper relations, and by way of apology?"

Michael considered for a moment, she was superior and cocky, but she was also sexy and asking him out for a drink. "Sure," he said, "I think could be arranged. Where do you fancy?"

"Why not the Crown? Everyone else seems to be going there."

Obscene Rituals

Bright golden sunlight washed through the open door and window of the Crown to ease out vapours of smoke, must, beer and earth into the air and roll around the sparsely populated volume of the lunchtime bar.

A figure moved through the gaseous soup, stirring it up and adding his own particular flavour of lemon scented aftershave and spearmint gum to its depths. He headed for the two tables pulled together in the corner and placed the five glasses in the middle of the nearest, leaving Jane to distribute them to their rightful owners as he left to retrieve his own. Returning, glass in hand, Michael raised it into the air. "Well here we are," he said, "Cheers."

"Cheers," the others chorused.

"So, David," Jane said. "You don't seem to approve of our Mr Balchin."

"If you mean that I don't appreciate someone making snap judgements about how informed or misinformed I am, you are correct."

"You did appear to know quite a lot about the historical background of the stones," Jane said.

David shrugged, "I have studied the period".

"It doesn't sound like a very good period," Jane said. "I certainly don't expect that many people, apart from the druids, would look back on those pre-Roman years and refer to them as the good old days."

"You might have liked them though," David said quietly, his downturned gaze flicking up briefly towards the reporter.

"Why?"

A simple question, with an answer in which all of the gathering was mildly interested, but David made them wait. He took a long pull at his beer, returned it to the table, and settled back on the sofa. No one broke the silence and David could feel the tension mounting—he let them off the hook: "You remind me of a description I read of Queen Boudica."

Jane failed to repress a laugh: "Do I take that as a compliment?"

"She's always reigned over me," Peter said, smiling.

David ignored him: "You may take it as a compliment others might not. Shall I tell you a story about her? It might also illustrate why I'm not too keen on the Celtic religion that Balchin admires and she followed."

"I'm always game for a good story," George said.

"Why not?" Jane said. "It will be nice to hear someone else's story."

"Okay. Are you sitting comfortably? Then I'll begin.

"In the days when the Romans occupied Britain, the populace of this sceptred isle was roughly split into three groups; the Druids, the warriors or fighting men, and the peasantry. It often took twenty years of training to become a fully-fledged Druid; they knew an awful lot about astronomy, and herbal medication, and were responsible for the religion, the dispensation of justice and teaching. However, they weren't just academics; if there was a dispute over leadership, and the normal voting did not work, then the matter was resolved by the sword.

"By AD 61 a lot of the Druidic holy places had been destroyed, and, it was just after Paulinus had wiped out a large rebel force in Anglesey, that news arrived of the death of the king of the Iceni, Prasutagus. He had hoped to save his kingdom from pillage by the army, by making the emperor Nero his joint heir along with his two daughters. But this didn't work: his wife, Boudica, was flogged, his two daughters raped and his chieftains stripped of their land.

"The Iceni were pretty annoyed and Boudica took charge of the army. Now it might have been hers to command anyway, because, before it was realised that there was a relationship between copulation and babies, the women were highly revered. Therefore, sovereignty was matrilinear, with the woman inheriting the title, marrying for a year and then sacrificing the husband, before choosing another. By Boudica's time though things had changed, but no one is sure by how much."

David glanced across at Jane: "That's why I said you might have liked those times."

"You're right. I might," Jane agreed.

"Anyway," David continued, "Boudica took charge of the army. Other tribes joined her, notably the Trinovates, and they gathered at her palace in Norfolk. There were over 100,000 men, and by the end of her campaign she commanded some 230,000." David took another sip of his beer and leant over the table—drawing the others in as his voice slipped into the hushed enveloping tone of the experienced storyteller. "There she stood, in front of her army; proud and tall, her mass of red hair, which fell down to her hips, flaring in the light from the rising sun, and her aspect glaring with anger at the injustices done to her and her family. She pointed the tip of her spear towards Colchester, home to the veterans of the hated Roman army; and, as the sun's light danced into the crowd from her spear tip and the twisted band of gold around her proud pale neck, they turned, and set off as one towards that hated city."

Jane's hand went involuntarily to the chain at her throat, and twisted the gold band around her fingers.

David paused briefly, enjoying the impatience that emanated from the others, and then continued. "When Boudica reached the city her men mingled with the town's population and spread word of fearful omens. The towns' folk were thrown into panic, and those who left then were the lucky ones. For when Boudica's army descended on the town, a few days later, the remaining population of 15,000 were massacred, and those that were captured were given up to mass sacrifice. One of the Druidic methods for doing this was to place the offenders in a massive wickerwork effigy, and, as the victims clawed over each other to climb further up the cage, its base was put to the torch. The flames rose higher and the screams of the victims floated higher still to be carried over the surrounding countryside.

"On this night it is said, although it is thought to be exaggerated, that some of the noblest of the women were hung up naked and then had their breasts cut off and sewn onto their lips; so that it looked as though they were eating their own flesh. They were then taken down and impaled on spikes in the sacred groves, from bottom to neck." David paused, and the silence was filled by the others returning their glasses to the table, and pushing away crisp packets.

"After that," David went on, more lightly, "Boudica's army left, hacked apart the Ninth Legion, that was on its way to relieve Colchester, and marched on London. They poured into London and the population of 30,000 never knew what had hit it. Even today, the Walbrook stream, which now runs underground, has been producing decapitated skulls, which were thought to have been an offering to the water spirit.

"Leaving the carnage of London behind her, Boudica marched on to meet her arch adversary, Suetonis. He was outnumbered ten to one, but he had strategically placed himself in a narrow defile with a wood at his back. Boudica rode at the head of her army, her two daughters flanking her; a constant reminder to her army of the injustices forced upon the people of Britain by the Romans. Inflamed as they were with hatred of the Romans and the thrill of recent victories, Boudica's army charged at their enemy as soon as they were sighted. Forced to attack Suetonis from the front, however, their battle cries soon turned to screams as his disciplined army cut right into the heart of their ranks. Boudica charged again and again into the fray, her red hair flying and her spear raised above her as she cut swathes through the Roman army; but, she failed. She survived the battle, but it is said that she took poison and committed suicide: unable to bear the fact that her once great army had been defeated and the people who had so depended on her were once again under the yoke of oppression."

The group were silent. David slumped back into the sofa, his glass cradled in his arms whilst the others hung their heads, and either stared at their glasses in contemplation or drank their contents for want of something to do.

"When did the Druids use the stone circles then?" Michael finally asked.

"On many occasions," David replied, placing his glass accurately back on the ring it had left on the table. "Oak trees were highly regarded, and they held many of their ceremonies in the clearings of oak forests and by water. But, quite often, it seems that they did use stone circles for their human sacrifices. You have got to remember though, that the Druids considered it quite an honour to be chosen as a sacrificial offering."

"Didn't they do anything at their ceremonies apart from sacrifice people?" Michael asked with something approaching exasperation. He was hoping to find some aspect of the religion that would not nauseate him and would support his prejudice that philosophers, from any age, must act more rationally than barbarically slaughtering people.

"Certainly," David replied. "They had many different feast days, and different ceremonies associated with each. For example, the four main annual feasts were, Imbolc, Beltane, Lughnasa and Samhuin; and on Beltane, for instance, they drove cattle between two fires as a symbolic offering to the sun.

"Another ritual has even filtered through to us today: the hanging of mistletoe above the door. The Celts cut it on the sixth day of the moon and hung it as a protection against evil."

"It sounds to me," Peter said, "that what they really needed was protection from their priests."

Michael grunted a laugh and looked across to Jane who had not spoken since the end of David's story. "Are you alright?" he asked.

"Huh?" Jane looked up, her eyes slightly glazed. She paused as though collecting her thoughts. "Yes. I think so. It just feels a little stuffy in here."

"Come on I'll take you outside. You just need a little air." Michael took her lightly by the arm. To his surprise, she rose, and without complaint or hesitation allowed him to walk her to the door.

"She probably needs something to settle her stomach after hearing that story of yours," Jonathan said, turning on David.

"I'm sorry, but I can't help the fact that I studied Celtic history. Even more to the point, I can't help it that history tends to be made up of gory details."

"You've got a point there," George agreed. "My grandfather only seemed to be able to tell me stories about farming accidents. I suppose it was to make sure I was careful on the farm. One story he told me ..."

Outside Michael lowered Jane onto the wooden bench, her back resting against the accompanying table, and squatted down in front of her. "And how do you feel now, Miss Appleby?" he asked.

As Jane's head tilted back to take in a deep breath her hand rose from the smooth depression of her skirt and brushed back the mane of red hair from her face. "I feel much better now. Thanks." She turned to look into his eyes. "Do you always help damsels in distress?" she asked.

"Only the beautiful ones. The dragons I leave to the dragon to take to bed on his hoard of gold."

"I'm glad you didn't think I was a dragon. Or are you just after my hoard of gold?"

"I'm not after any gold. But I know that you're chasing my story," he replied.

Jane laughed. "Your story? Haven't you found out yet that finders aren't necessarily keepers?"

"No, perhaps I haven't," he grunted, rising to his feet. "Anyway, if you're feeling better shall I escort you back to the others?"

"Yes. Thank you," Jane said, taking his proffered hands.

His grasp was tight and Jane winced as he hauled her to her feet, but he quickly relinquished his grip and bent to kiss her hand.

Jane smiled sweetly. "The last lips to touch that hand belonged to one of George's cows," she said, starting back towards the pub.

Noxious Fumes

The door swung open on its shiny hinges, and it was as though it had opened the way into an Egyptian tomb. There was no visible reason for this; everything in the room was spotlessly clean and almost new. It was the smell that did it: a dank, mouldering, heavy smell, which seemed to owe its substance to the weight of ages.

Physiologists tell that the sense of smell, although one of our least sophisticated senses, has the ability to conjure up the most vivid memories and stir the greatest of emotions. In Marian's case, this scent stirred up the instinct to run, to turn around and escape from the feeling that death was trailing his cloak under her nose and wrapping the mind numbing tendrils of his breath around her mind.

"Phew it's a bit pongy, isn't it?" her mother said, from behind her.

Marian backed into her. "Come on. Let's just get out of here and close the door. I'll think about what to do with it later," she said, trying not to breathe in the foetid air.

"You've said that before and you still haven't done anything. You can't leave it forever you know," her mother replied, slipping past her and into the room.

"I don't intend to, I just want to get out of here now."

"But you haven't found out where the smell is coming from yet."

"I don't care."

"Well let's, at least, open the outside door to air it."

Mrs Stanton went over to the large roll-down door, twisted the handle, and heaved it upwards. The fresh air fell into the room so possessively that it was almost audible, but, although the stench had been dismissed, the overall feeling of heavy gloom still hung on tenaciously.

"Where do you think the smell is coming from?" her mother asked, looking around her. "The walls don't seem to be damp."

"I would imagine it's the stone."

"Why?" her mother asked, going over to the accused. "It's not damp either. Come and feel it."

"I don't want to."

"Come on. It's not going to bite you, it hasn't me."

Driven partly by curiosity, Marian went over to the stone and very cautiously laid her hand against it. The stone felt dry and cold, but something else as well. A thrill of uncertain surprise temporarily accosted her, similar to that experienced when drinking coffee and expecting tea—familiar but unexpected. Then, as she continued to touch it, the stone felt cold, it felt rain-washed, she felt rain-washed, tied to it: wet jeans clinging to her legs, the stone pushing up between her encircling arms and bound legs. However, whereas the stone felt cold, she felt warm, and a fluid glow burst into being, flowing from her groin to her feet and head and striking each nerve ending it passed, into acute awareness.

"Marian!" her mother cried. "Are you alright?"

Marian looked up to discover that her arms were wrapped around the stone, hugging it tightly. "Err, yes. I'm fine," she said, disengaging herself. "I. Err. I just needed to support myself. I felt a little faint."

"It's the air in here. That's what it is," Mrs Stanton said. "Come on let's get you back into the house and I'll make you a nice cup of tea, and you can have some of my home made shortbread."

"Home made? It doesn't feel much like a home, without John here."

"Well do any of us have a true home?" her mother asked, putting an arm around her. "We all move around so much these days. We call a place home for a time, move on and then call somewhere else by the same name."

"I suppose home is where the heart is," Marian said, forlornly, "or where you spent your childhood."

The stone standing impassively behind her had stood for several thousand years in the same spot. It was far from home.

Everything's Going To Be Alright

"Is there anything I can get you love?"

"No thanks," Danny replied. "I'd just like to get out of bed and walk around."

"I know you would," his mother said, sympathetically. "But you can't do that just yet. You have to allow your bones to heal first. It's a bit like a jigsaw down there you know. I saw the X-rays."

"I know; so did I," Danny said, "but it is going to get better isn't it?" his voice pleaded.

"Yes of course it is." His mother came and sat on the edge of his bed and pushed his fair hair away from his troubled eyes. "You're just going to have to give it time, follow the doctors' instructions and rest for a while. You know you should try to sleep more. One moment you do nothing but sleep, and the next it's all we can do to get you to rest your head for a few minutes."

"I don't want to sleep."

"Why not?"

"Because when I do, I have horrible dreams and when I wake up my wrists hurt."

Mrs Jones gently picked up her son's right hand and turned it over to look at the wrist. "Yes," she said, "those marks don't seem to have gone down much. It is peculiar. But tell me about these nightmares, what do you dream about?"

"I don't know. It's not like a normal dream, where you can see things happening; all I can see is darkness and all I can feel is cold. But I can't breathe and I know there is something else there with me."

"What sort of thing?"

"I don't know, I can't see it."

"Does this thing hurt you?"

"No it doesn't and it doesn't feel bad. It just doesn't want me there and I know it doesn't like me being there. I can't breathe and it pushes me out into the open, which is when I wake up."

"Does it take hold of you then?" Mrs Jones was trying to think of some explanation for Danny's aching wrists.

"No, it's more like when you get two magnets and they push each other away. I just feel this pressure on me and then it gets more and more, and I start moving upwards, faster and faster, until I hit the light. And then there's light all around me and it hurts."

"Does this happen every time you go to sleep?"

"Yes. And when the room is dark I can sometimes feel it in the room with me."

Mrs Jones could tell that the recollections were disturbing her son and she gently cupped his hand in hers. "Well I'll tell you what we'll do then shall I? I'll make the camp bed up in here and your father and I will take it in turns to sleep in here with you. That way you'll know that the only horrible thing in the room with you is your dad's feet."

Danny smiled at her. "Thanks," he said. "That will be great, but I still won't want to go to sleep."

"We'll see," his mother said, getting up. "But to make your captivity a little easier, I'll ask your dad to bring the television up to you when he comes home."

"What will you watch?"

"We'll come and watch with you."

"But it's too big for him to carry, mum."

"He once said that when he had to carry me over the threshold," his mother smiled, "but when I clipped him around the ear he soon found he had hidden strengths."

Stone Love

The car slowly turned the corner, its engine barely ticking over, until it reached the hump-backed bridge. There it accelerated and its headlights seared into the night sky, proclaiming the car's presence for a brief instant, before they returned to earth and were dimmed on reunion with the tarmac.

The engine was cut—allowing the river's muttered sighs to reclaim their dominion.

One, two, three, ten heartbeats, a steadying held breath, and then a heavy clunk announced the car door opening. A pair of long legs uncoiled and cut into the damp night air; probing the moist ground. Assured that the terrain was safe, the rest of the body followed, and Jane turned towards the field. Before her was the shield of the stone wall, but behind it lay a much larger and more intriguing member of its kind.

Uncertainly she approached the barrier and looked over. The stone reared up from the black backdrop of the night, a bright shroud of moonlight dipped moisture gleaming on its surface, and it beckoned to her.

To look had been her intent, to see and remember, an urge she had not understood, but now she needed to touch, as Thomas had his saviour, to confirm, to understand, to know.

Alone on the road, a solitary visitor, she wedged the pointed toe of her shoe into the gap formed by the wall's binding stones, and heaved herself upwards. Expensive veneer was removed, torn back from the shoe, but it was ignored by the primitive drive that impelled her over the wall and towards her goal.

Received with open arms, the cold moist surface of the monolith chilled her caress—Braille like pits, troughs and ridges whispering past the sensitive pads of her fingers, telling their story of age as she trailed her hand along its surface. However, it was a story she could not read, and she turned and slumped back against the stone, seeking for answers to her presence as she raised her face to the moon.

David's words rang through her head in harmonic resonance. She could picture the scene his tale had painted: the fires blazing high, the orgiastic victory celebrations of Boudica's army, the smell of smoke and roast meats floating from the fires, the shouts of revelry, and amongst it all, standing proudly, Boudica. Or, was it herself?

Arms stretched behind to touch the stone's grey security, head flung back, face pointed to the sky, her closed eyelids and parted lips were the first to feel the pearls of rain and she saw herself standing on a storm-ridden battlefield. Broken bodies lay all around, a bleeding red carpet of success for her army, who ran across it, shouting with joy as they carried her in victory. A victory of blood. Blood, which spilled down her arms in pink rivulets, diluted by the cleansing rain, and dripped onto the heads and upturned faces of her bearers.

In furious waves the cheering and the smell of the rain soaked, blood sodden ground rose about her, filling her senses, dominating her will and enveloping her in their own reality, refuting her own. She looked up across the heads of the screaming mob, looking for an exit, and saw an anachronism. An anachronism that refused denial, no matter how she tried to fit it into her situation. Someone else was approaching her through the revel of her army: Michael Thornton; but, unlike the others, he wasn't dressed in ancient Briton costume, just his normal, brown suit and raincoat. He reached out to touch her—an open palm of friendship. Her fingers stretched and, contact. She was ripped back to reality, finding herself clenched to the stone, rain coursing down her body, trickling into her mouth and down her neck. She opened her eyes. There was no army about her, no battlefield and no Michael Thornton, but she remained clinging to the stone, aware that something had changed. Everything had changed. She saw, felt, appreciated that there was a history and a meaning in all the elements of her surroundings. They pressed in against her, engorged by their new meaning, filling in the space, demanding her attention. The grass, no longer a mere damp blanket to be trodden, but a collection of living individuals, each blade a different shade in the turn of the breeze; fifty, sixty different types, planted, trodden, nourished, eaten—descendants of the original grasses which had dominated the land before man. The air, merely fresh before, was now packed with a hundred individual scents, each as clear as the moon in a cloudless sky. The stone, rearing up behind her, refusing denial, but telling a tale she did not wish to know. She released her grip and plunged forward. A leap, a run and a step, and she saved herself from the ground, but it was still some time before she managed to stagger back to the wall.

Steam drifted up from her clothes as she slumped back into the driver's seat. Too shaken to drive she switched on the radio and reflected on her experience. Interesting though it had been, it was not one that she would willingly repeat.

Trick With A Stick

The rough bark dug into Marian's back as she leant against the tree's support and peered from beneath the parasol of leaves at the blue sky above. A few white wispy clouds were all that remained of the weekend's dark squadrons, whose hit and run bombing campaigns had made her rush for cover. Two days of sunshine had made all the difference: the ground was dry, the spring flowers were coming into bloom and the feeling of despair had, for a moment, evaporated from her shoulders. A smile even brightened her eyes when the cloth-capped old man once more crossed her line of vision—his twitching stick held before him.

"No luck, Mr Dart?" she called.

The old man lowered his arms and removed his cap to reveal a dark sweep of perspiration stained hair. "No. I just can't seem to find the root of the problem," he complained.

"Why is that?" Mrs Stanton asked with concern.

"Yes, why is that?" Marian probed with mischievous delight. "After all, you were the one who told us we had a problem."

"It's not that I don't know you have a problem. I do; it's obvious," frustration moulded the droop of his shoulders. "It's just that I can't seem to find the source, because it appears to be all around us. It's as though the house and grounds are sitting on a vast underground lake or a network of small streams."

"That sounds quite serious," Mrs Stanton said. "Which do you think it is, Alfred?"

The diviner looked up from his dejection with a reassuring smile. "Don't worry, I don't think you are sitting on an underground lake, and I can definitely detect lines running to, or from, the site."

"How intriguing," Marian said, grinning up at the diviner. "So what's the next step or twitch you're going to take, Mr Dart?"

"I think I should try inside the house now," Mr Dart replied. "That's where everything seems to point to."

"All roads led to Rome and all streams lead to our house, eh?" Marian said, getting up.

"Well hopefully not all, Mrs Dally."

"Come on then, Alfred," Mrs Stanton said. "Let's see if you can find the source of our Nile."

Marian looked curiously at her mother who was practically skipping into the house. It was clear that she was enjoying all of this and Marian was not at all sure that her mother did not have a crush on Mr Dart. It was difficult to contemplate that her mother might just be starting a relationship as hers had finished.

She wandered back towards the house, deep in thought, and paused to cut some flowers. Scissors in hand, blades encompassing the stem of a daffodil, she stopped short of executing the decapitation, painful, stupid guilt telling her that she would be causing the cessation of life.

Empty handed she entered the house and met Alfred Dart emerging from the dining room. "Have you discovered where the bottom of our well is?" she asked.

"No, but I have narrowed it down. I'll check the kitchen now, if I may."

"Fine, you go ahead," Marian said. "I'll wait here." She looked down and saw that Mr Dart's dog, Bess, was sitting by the doorway to John's studio.

"Hello girl, what are you doing then?" She bent down and ruffled the dog's thick fur with both hands, slowly slipping the luxuriant coat between her fingers, using the glossy strands as worry beads to ease her thoughts.

"It looks like Bess got here before me."

Marian looked up. Mr Dart was standing next to her, the Y shaped stick twisted in his hands so that its stem was lying against his chest, pointing to his face. "Do you think it's in here then?" she asked quietly.

"It looks that way."

With a sigh Marian rose and opened the door; opened it to what she had always known and feared would be the inevitable end of the trail.

She stepped back. Having told her mother not to mention the stone to Mr Dart, she had wondered how the diviner would react when confronted with it. As it happened, he did nothing. Bess, on the other hand, slipped past her master and trotted over to lie, curled against the stone.

Without saying a word, Mr Dart slowly raised his stick, carefully tensed his wrists and took a step forward. Immediately the stick kicked upwards to slap against his chest; its dull thud accompanied by Marian catching her breath, startled by the ferocity of its movement.

Alfred Dart brought the stick back under control and continued forward, his slow steady transepts across the room, constantly accompanied by the stick twisting and jumping in his hand as though it was some writhing creature trying to escape his grasp. Finally, the journey ended, he stood next to his dog and the stone, the switch of ash hanging motionless at his side. "This is it," he said. "This, or something directly underneath it."

Marian, standing in the doorway, could do nothing but nod her head.

Her mother came up behind her to lay a comforting hand on her shoulder.

"What is it?" Mr Dart asked, gazing up at the towering monolith.

"It belonged to my husband," Marian said. "It was going to be a statue."

"A statue of what?"

"He hadn't really decided. He was considering making it into a fountain."

"Was it almost finished?" Mr Dart asked with some doubt.

"No. He hadn't even started on it yet. He was hoping to begin the day," Marian stopped and swallowed carefully. "The day after the accident."

Mr Dart paused, sensing Marian's discomfort. He wanted to respect her feelings, but he needed answers. Marian and her mother needed answers.

"Where did he get the stone from?"

"I'm not sure exactly. He saw it in a field near Penzance when he was visiting a friend, and he bought it from the farmer."

Alfred Dart stared at her, a possibility suddenly dawning on him. He turned back to the stone and ran his hand slowly over the rock. "Is this the stone that was lost from the stone circle?" he asked quietly, addressing the stone more than anyone else.

"I don't know," Marian said, shrugging her shoulders, "I don't know of any missing stone."

"Don't you read the papers?"

"Not recently, no," her mother answered, becoming defensive on her daughters behalf. "We have had other things to keep our minds occupied."

"I'm sorry," Mr Dart apologised, "but I thought you would have heard. There's a hunt going on for a stone that was part of a circle, but which was sold to some unknown buyer."

"Well I don't think it could be this stone," Marian said. "John never mentioned a stone circle."

"It could be though," the diviner persisted, "all the other stones were very small; so they couldn't be seen easily."

"I don't know," Marian said, shaking her head. "But, come to think of it, he did say that there was another smaller stone across the river from it."

"That's it then. It must be the same one, because they say in the paper that a stone, similar to the missing one, was moving to try and fill in the gap left by its larger partner."

"Moving?" Mrs Stanton laughed.

"That's what they said in the papers," Mr Dart replied.

Marian studied the stone, "Have you still got the paper that the story was in?"

"Yes I put it in my cuttings file."

"Do you think I could look at it sometime?"

"Certainly."

"Do you think our stone and that mentioned in the paper might be one and the same then?" Mrs Stanton asked her daughter.

"No. It's probably just a coincidence. I'm just interested."

"What if it is the same stone though," Alfred Dart said, bending down to ruffle Bess's head. "What will you do then?"

Overcast By A Premonition

The glass turned slowly in George's hand, its base quietly grating on the wooden tabletop. Fizzled away with time, the head on the pint of bitter had all but disappeared, and its level indicated a certain lack of interest in its depths.

It was early for George to be in the pub, so when Gerry came in, Linda expressed her concern to the tall librarian as she pulled his pint.

"He's just been sitting there: not drinking, not speaking. He didn't even speak to me much; just ordered his beer. What do you think can be the matter?"

"I've no idea," Gerry replied, turning round to look at George, "He seemed to be perfectly alright yesterday, but it does look as if he wants to be left alone. Perhaps I shouldn't intrude just yet; he can always come and speak to me if he wants to." He took a sip of the beer that Linda had placed in front of him, and savoured the dark hoppy taste as it slipped down. Smacking his lips in appreciation, he turned at the sound of the door opening behind him.

It was Barney; raising his hand in general greeting as he plodded over to stand next to Gerry at the bar: "A pint of Hick's please, Linda," he ordered. He pivoted on his elbow and spotted George sitting in the corner. "Hi! George," he called over, "what's the matter with you then?"

George looked up as Gerry bowed his head and muttered oaths.

"Nothing," George replied, putting a smile on his face.

"Can I get you another drink then?"

George looked at his glass as though faintly surprised that it was still there: "Err, yes I will have another. Thanks."

Barney turned back to the bar, "Make that two pints, Linda."

"What about you, Gerry, do you want another? It looks as though you could do with one. Last time I saw a face like that it had bitten a maggot."

Gerry turned slowly on his companion: "The reason why my brow was so furrowed, was that I was wondering if you knew anything more about the word 'tact', other than it being a word that lies in the dictionary, somewhere between sensitive and unfeeling. I decided that you didn't."

"I'm sorry?" Barney said, in puzzlement.

"I just thought," Gerry said lowering his voice, "that it appeared as if, George wanted to be alone with his thoughts."

"Oh well; if he's feeling a bit down he'll want us to cheer him up, won't he? Come on."

"Perhaps you're right," Gerry sighed resignedly, picking up his glass and following.

"How are things then, George?" Barney asked, sitting down next to him.

"Fine, fine," he replied.

"How about your historians," Gerry asked. "Have they discovered anything yet?"

"Well they seem to be getting along alright. I don't think that they have found anything. Although they say that the evidence does point towards it being a genuine circle."

"Well that's good news isn't it?" Barney said.

"Yes I suppose so. It means that it's more likely that I'll be allowed to keep my land."

"Have you spoken to the council yet? To that woman, whatever her name was." Gerry's asked, struggling to undo the small bow-tie at his throat.

"Heather Mason? Yes, I've spoken to her, and I didn't like her. She sounded a right snobby little piece of work."

"Didn't she offer you any advice then?" Gerry asked, still fighting with the tie that appeared to be wrapped around his neck with the tenacity of a starving anaconda.

"She did say," George started slowly, fascinated by the struggle unfolding before him, "that having had no official complaint from me, the plans were going through according to schedule. But that they were willing to let the matter rest whilst they awaited the findings of these investigations." He ended his sentence in a rush, keeping pace with Gerry's exertions, and finished in time to see the tie hanging limply from Gerry's hand.

"What! You haven't sent in an official objection." Gerry's long face was a crimson mixture of exertion and emotion. He ran a finger under his collar. "Why ever not?"

"I don't know," Barney said. "What's the use of trying to help people who won't help themselves?"

"I just didn't seem to have the time, what with all the normal farm business to run, and all this trouble with the stones," George said. "But I will try and get one written up soon."

"You better had," Gerry said. "Do you want me to help you with it?"

"No, but thank you for the offer. I should have a bit more time now that Harry's coming back."

A silence can sometimes filter through the air as quickly and possessively as a crash of thunder; and that's what happened now. A Chinese whisper passed around the room and silence followed in its wake, splitting apart companions and snuffing out conversation, until all that could be heard was the swishing of beer into a pint glass.

Gerry coughed, "Well that will be nice for you won't it?" he said, "When is he coming back?"

"In two days time," George said. "I got his letter this morning."

"Does he know about the stone?" Barney asked.

"No."

"What do you think he'll say?" Barney asked, trying to sound casual as his big fingers twisted around his glass.

"I haven't any idea." George said, relaxing his shoulders, and thinking, what will he say?

Neolithic Ingenuity

As the breeze sifted through the grass, it levered the hot, heavily scented, air from its green cushion and brushed it through George's greying hair. Leaning over the gate into his small field he tilted his head back and revelled in the caress of the warm fragrant waves; the cows behind him munching on their grass, content after their morning milking and the sun warm on the back of his neck—easing his muscles and flinging the shadows of the industrious archaeologists out towards the road and the towering hill. The term 'a hive of activity' sprang to George's mind, its aptness obvious: each individual, although engrossed in their own project, would occasionally leave their task to meet up with another, and then move on; as if weaving an intricate dance to depict the location of a hidden prize. He watched with objective detachment, the panic of his ruse being discovered temporarily quelled by the serenity of his surroundings. His eyes wandered along the line of the shadows and saw David's blue car roll over the bridge, and turn into the entrance of his yard. With a sigh, he turned back towards the house—serenity could be so short lived.

"Hi George," Jonathan called, climbing out of the car. "How's things?"

George was stunned. "I'm alright," he replied, "but what about you? Have you got ring worm or something?"

Jonathan's response was indignant: "I beg your pardon?"

David laughed: "George is referring to our haircuts. If you had ring worm, the remedy was to shave the hair and paint the surface of the skin with a vile purple liquid."

"Oh, I see," Jonathan grunted. "Well you can rest at ease, George. We have no intention of painting our heads; we simply decided to have crew cuts for the summer." He brushed the top of his head with his hand. "But it does feel nice. Go on have a feel." He bent his head, and George tentatively held out his hand.

"It feels like suede," was George's verdict.

"That's us; a couple of suede heads," David laughed.

"What are you up to anyway?" Jonathan asked George.

"Actually I'm just waiting for my cement to arrive, so that I can start on the foundations for my new hen house."

"Do you need any help?" David asked.

"Well if you're around I wouldn't mind a hand, but I don't want to put you out."

"Don't worry we'll stop when we've had enough," Jonathan said. "How is the research going anyway?"

"I don't know, I haven't spoken to them this morning. Shall we go and find out?"

Assenting they set off across the field towards Balchin and his crew, George taking up the central position, but it wasn't the ex-druid who George had his eye upon, but rather John the engineer. For it was John, the very man who could prove that the stone's movements were faked, who George had seen suddenly squatting down to examine the riverbank.

"Good morning Mr Penton," Balchin said at their approach.

"Morning," George responded. "How are your investigations coming along?"

"Quite well." Balchin turned to place his clipboard on the small trestle table, which had been erected near the site of the absent stone. "It would appear that these stones aren't in their natural form but have been shaped."

"Is that good?" George asked.

"It could be Mr Penton. The stones are granite, which means that they are very hard. Therefore, the person, or persons, who shaped them, must have been dedicated to their task. The kind of dedication that is normally found only in the construction of ritual artefacts."

"Couldn't they have been shaped more recently though?" David asked

"Admittedly that is true," Balchin said, his enthusiasm overcoming his distaste for David. "But there are other circles in this area whose constituent stones are also granite and which have been crafted in a similar manner."

"Where are they?" Jonathan asked.

The swaying commenced. Hands clasped behind him, eyes closed, the flapping corners of Balchin's tweed jacket did nothing to detract from his vulturine image. "Bodmin Moor," he replied. "There are several circles situated there, including 'The Hurlers'. Local superstition has it that these stones are men who were turned to stone for hurling the ball on the Lords day," a half smile twitched at the corner of his mouth. "But it is there that we also find that some of the granite stones have been smoothed by hammering, and that the brittle splinters, by-products of the process, were spread around the interior of the circle as a crude form of paving."

"Sounds like hard work," Jonathan said.

Balchin stopped his weaving and opened his eyes. His glare locked onto Jonathan's hair, as if noticing it for the first time. "Yes," he replied, frowning, "but they weren't afraid of hard work, in those days. It must have taken over one and a half million man hours merely to dig the pit around the sandstone circle at Avebury, never mind erecting the actual stones."

"They took their time then," Jonathan said, returning Balchin's stare.

"They only had deer antlers and stones to dig with," Balchin coldly informed him.

"Quite a feat of engineering then." George said with admiration.

"Oh indeed," Balchin's tone immediately warmed again with enthusiasm, "and when you consider that they had to transport the Sarsen stones, which weighed in the region of thirty tons, over a distance of twenty miles; you begin to fully realize the enormity of the task." A silence ensued and whether Balchin gave any credit to his audience's perspicacity was difficult to tell, because he quickly went on to elaborate: "Some of the stones weighed as much as forty seven tons you see, and the breaking strain of their best ropes was only one third of a ton."

"How did they do it then?" Jonathan asked.

"Lots of ropes," David answered.

"Yes," Balchin said, looking slightly piqued that David had pipped him to the post. "What they were able to achieve, without using machines has proved to be quite amazing. Near Stonehenge, thirty-two teenage boys were able to pull a sledge up a slope carrying a stone weighing one and a half tons. It was estimated that each boy had a pull equivalent to one hundred and ten pounds over a short distance. I bet you two would have liked to have been there to see that," He remarked with a sly glance at Jonathan.

"It was also found," he quickly continued, "that, in the Sandalwood Islands, five hundred natives could pull an eleven ton block of stone for a distance of two miles."

"Just goes to show that some people have more pulling power than others," David commented. "I bet you keep people enthralled at parties with your knowledge of little known facts. Have you been invited to any parties recently, Mr Balchin?"

Balchin bestowed a stately smile on his antagonist.

George stepped into the rift. "Have you been able to find out how old our circle is yet?" he asked.

Balchin turned his back on David to address George directly "No, I'm afraid not. We have no reliable way of actually measuring the age of the stones at the moment. Lethbridge did hold a pendulum close to some stone circles to measure their age by counting the number of gyrations made by the pendulum, but we don't exactly consider that conclusive proof.

"Our one hope in that direction is that Mark may discover deposits of organic material around the stones. It was quite a feature of many of the circles to find such pits filled with domestic refuse, and this can be carbon dated."

"Excuse me may I interrupt for a moment?" It was John who had come up from the riverbank to join the group. "If you want to hear some news I think I can supply it," he said. "I haven't found out how the stone moved yet, but I'll tell you this; the river has moved."

"What!" George exclaimed. "By how much?"

"Not much, but it might still be moving. It's moving towards the stone and away from this field."

George stared at the man in open disbelief. He knew that there had been something odd about the riverbank, but what was happening? Was this good news or bad news? Was someone playing a joke on him? He needed time to think. He needed space.

Walking towards the group Michael Thornton knew nothing of the recent turn of events, all he saw was George stalking towards him across the field.

"Mr Penton," he tried as George drew level, "how are you?" but he received no reply, just a grunt as George passed by.

Michael looked after him, puzzled. George was usually one of the most amicable people he knew, something must have upset him. He turned back towards the group and saw Jonathan and David approaching. "Like the haircuts," Michael approved. "What's the matter with him?"

"I don't know," David said, "But rumour has it that his son, Harry, is about to come home."

"So what's wrong with that? I'd have thought he would be pleased."

"Well he would be normally, but not under the present circumstances. He hasn't told Harry that he's sold the stone."

"Is that so bad?"

"Don't you know the story about Harry?" David's eyebrows rose in surprise. "No I don't suppose you do. You haven't been here very long have you?"

"It's been two years," Michael bridled.

"It's not long enough," David informed him. "It is an interesting story; but no one would thank you for printing it."

"Why?"

"They just wouldn't."

"You can't just leave me hanging in the air. Tell me the story."

"Not here and not now, but buy us a pint and I might."

Eulogy Of The Past

Breakfast was David's favourite meal of the day, especially after a heavy drinking session like that of the previous night. So, he was grateful that his mother had especially prepared a late breakfast for them, and pleasantly surprised that she had considerately laid places for them on the bare kitchen table, away from the clamour of the leaving guests.

The whole ensemble of bacon, sausage, tomatoes, egg, fried bread and mushrooms was, as usual, cooked to perfection, and David was not the only grateful recipient. Jonathan wiped his lips with the pink and white checked napkin and pushed his empty plate away from him with obvious delight. "Thank you for the meal Mrs Pengelly," he congratulated. "That was lovely."

"Glad you liked it," she replied. "What are you two intending to do today?"

"Jonathan was thinking of going to Marazion to paint St Mike's Mount, and I thought I'd go along and watch," David said, getting up to clear the table.

"With those haircuts, the only painting you look like you'd do is graffiti on bus shelters. I don't know why you let Jonathan persuade you to have it done, David, I really don't. It looks awful."

Seeing Jonathan's jaw drop in disbelief from the corner of his eye, David hurriedly explained: "You must have misunderstood me, Mum," he blurted, feeling Jonathan's gaze follow him around the kitchen. "I just happened to mention that I liked someone's haircut, and Jonathan said that it would suit me."

"I'm surprised that he makes any money as an artist if he has taste like that then," his mother said, getting up from the kitchen table.

Jonathan was beginning to feel like he had ceased to exist in the room.

"Well obviously some people like his work," David said.

"Oh thanks," Jonathan huffed.

"I didn't mean it to sound like that. I was merely suggesting that your work must be good for all those corporations and institutions to have your paintings on their walls."

"What do you mean institutions?" his mother asked, "Do you mean mental hospitals?"

"No, of course I don't. Mind you," David continued, thoughtfully, "there is that one isn't there? The one that... Jonathan? Jonathan!" Jonathan had made his exasperated exit.

"I suppose that's meant to be his artistic temperament coming out," Mrs Pengelly said, filling up the kettle.

"Quite possibly," David said, closing the door to the dishwasher. "By the way, don't bother making dinner tonight; we thought we would cook for you for a change."

"Oh that's nice of you. What are we having?"

"I don't know," he replied, placing the blue and white teacups on the table. "It was actually Jonathan's idea. It will be a surprise."

"The meal went down quite well, I thought," David said, as they drove out of town.

"Yes it was a nice piece of beef," Jonathan said, lolling his head back on the headrest.

"Mind you, I think my mother was a bit worried when I told her you were going to be cooking a surprise meal for her. She probably thought that you intended to poison her."

"Maybe that's why she kept peering over my shoulder; to see if I'd laced the meat with Cyanide."

"Or perhaps she just wanted to see if you had put any garlic in it," David suggested.

They continued driving whilst the bushes, which formed their ragged guard of honour, held back long rays from the day's exhausted sun and cast their deformed images onto the cloying surface of the warm tarmac. Caught between the flickers of light and shade as he drove David's eyes began to water and with thumb and forefinger he tried to wipe away the haze, but to no permanent avail, and was grateful when he saw the bulk of their destination appear in an oasis of dark shade. He turned the car off the road and into the gravelled car park, where the black stones crunching under their wheels were tinged with purple from a bright sign hanging below the eaves of the adjacent building.

Jonathan read the garish sign. "'The Old Mill'," he said. "What is this a public house or a pizza parlour?"

"It's an out of the way pub where it will be possible to conduct a private conversation," David said, drawing the car to a halt.

Jonathan undid his safety belt and looked out through the car window. "I suppose that was obvious really," he said. "After all, once you've seen that sign, you're not likely to hold down any meal for long."

David yawned and got out of the car—his friend's cynical humour could be a little wearing at times, and the yawn was a signal he knew Jonathan would not miss.

Michael Thornton had arrived before them. Ensconced in the angle of the stone wall and the wooden staircase, he was sitting on a rattan chair with a steel tipped weaving shuttle hanging from the wall above his head. He signalled for them to join him, and they sank into the two-seater sofa opposite him. David peered over his raised knees in surprise as a pint glass was brought over by the barmaid and placed in front of him. "That's quick work," he commented.

"I ordered them for you," Michael said. "Some people don't like to waste valuable drinking time, but I don't like to waste interviewing time. I do hope this isn't going to be a waste of mine."

"No it shouldn't be," David replied. "I don't doubt for an instant that you will find what I have to say very interesting, although, as I implied earlier, the locals would not appreciate you for printing the story."

"I've already had some proof of the truth behind that statement."

"Oh?"

"I asked my editor if he knew anything about the secret life of George Penton's son, and he told me that he did. That, however, was the way he intended it to remain: he wasn't going to tell me what he knew and he said I shouldn't investigate it any further."

"It doesn't surprise me," David said. "It's a close knit community around here, and they don't want old wounds re-opened."

"Well come on then," Jonathan urged. "Stop building the tension and tell the story. You're not Hercule Poirot in a room of suspects; tell us who did it."

The turn of David's head was enough of a signal for Jonathan to gauge the mood of his friend and he sank his lips into his frothy pint and stared at the table as though it were the most fascinating piece of furniture he had ever seen.

A silence settled around the table, as David took a sip of his beer and returned the glass to the ring it had left on the table. "When Harry Penton was about thirteen years old," he began, "there was a girl who played with him and his friends called Sarah Nancarrow. When I say played with them I mean just that. She was older than they were by three years, and she took advantage of this by acting as a woman of the world, who'd seen it all, done it all, and could show them how to do the same.

"I know all this because I had recently come to the area and went to the same school as they did, but, as I was the new boy in town, they wouldn't speak to me and I saw it all from the outside.

"Harry was a big lad and, as such, he was the natural leader of the gang, or so he thought. Sarah was the power behind the throne; whatever she decided on a whim became the goal of the gang, and Harry deluded himself that it had been his decision.

Sarah had only been in the town for two years, but she had already gained a reputation as a hell raiser who would do anything to be noticed. Her parents had both died in a house fire, which she had survived, and she had been sent here to live with her grandparents. Unfortunately they couldn't control her—she landed in trouble with the school for truancy, the police for car theft and the suspected arson of a local barn."

Michael raised his eyebrows at this revelation, but he knew better than to interrupt a storyteller in mid flow, so he sipped his drink and sat back in his chair.

Jonathan continued to stare at the table.

"Once she became involved with Harry's gang she quietened down a bit," David continued, "but by then she had found out about the stones on Harry's land, and, in retrospect, it seems as though she was just trying to ingratiate herself with the gang and lull them into a false sense of security.

"One afternoon I watched them from the hill across from the farm. Sarah seemed to be playing the part of High Priestess and Harry her chief assistant. They had caught a rabbit and, whilst the others held it down on the ground in what I now know to be the centre of the circle, Sarah slit it open from top to bottom allowing Harry to take out its entrails and dab the group's faces with the blood. I seem to remember that they didn't look too happy about that.

"When he'd finished he draped the entrails around the large stone and Sarah came forward wiped her hands all over them and the stone, and turned round to pull down Harry's pants, and rub her blood smeared hands on him. She then enacted the same ritual with the other four, dare I say, members of the gang?"

Jonathan looked in astonishment at his friend. "You watched all this?"

"Afraid so," David replied. "Would you have turned away?" He smiled. "I wanted to know what they did at their meetings, so I borrowed my father's binoculars and spied on them. And, although I must admit to being a little excited by what I saw, it did reinforce my doubts about abandoning myself to a female's sexuality."

The others said nothing; Michael merely took another drink and waited for the silence to exhaust itself.

"It was the way she smiled," David eventually continued, "it wasn't the look of someone enjoying a sexual experience. It was the gloating smile of someone in total control, and enjoying the power they could exert over inferiors." David shook his head to clear his thoughts and took another gulp of his dying beer. "Anyway," he said, looking up, "it appears as if she may have over reached herself. She disappeared shortly afterwards, and it was generally accepted that she died. The police found traces of her blood on the stone, the one that George has now sold, and when they interviewed Harry he told a very interesting story. Apparently, the evening before her disappearance Sarah had told the boys to tie her to the stone. She had worn an especially long white dress for the occasion, and once she was trussed up, they sacrificed yet another unfortunate rabbit. Then, on Sarah's instructions, they sacrificed her. Harry didn't want to do it, but she kept on taunting him and telling him that if he was a real man, instead of a little boy, he would do it; so he cut her wrists. Harry and the others insisted that she survived; she had screamed when they cut her and then screamed even louder to be cut free. As soon as they released her they say she ran off, but she was never seen again.

"Of course the police investigated the incident thoroughly, but without a body there wasn't much they could do to the boys.

"The lads, and especially Harry, were under suspicion from the village for a long time, but, privately, many of the villagers thought that Sarah Nancarrow was a girl who was seeking the end which befell her, whatever it may have been."

Sapient Wood?

"You look stupid mother."

Marian's mother was standing in the doorway, a light rain coat buttoned up to her neck, a clear, pink tinted, plastic rain hood pulled over her blue permed hair, and two plastic pen cases held in her hands. The insides of these had been removed, and, in their place, two pieces of coat hanger wire had been inserted, which had been bent over at ninety degrees, so that when the pen case handles were held vertically the wire stretched out for about a foot, parallel to the ground, and could rotate within their handles.

"Alfred said I could use these as a divining rod," Mrs Stanton coolly replied. "And, because he said that there is too much energy in here for me to pick up a directional reading, I am going outside to test it."

"But it's raining." If Stanley had said to Livingston, 'There's a man eating lion outside the tent, why do you have to go for a walk now?' He could not have sounded more bemused than Marian.

"That," her mother stated, "is why I am wearing my rain hood. And I do hope that you are going to write that letter while I'm out."

"Yes, I'm just about to do it now," Marian sighed resignedly. "I'm just not sure about where to send it."

"Send it to him care of the farm. That's where he's been working; the address will be in the telephone directory and, let's face it, there can't be any harm in just writing to him, so get on with it." She adjusted the strings on her rain hood. "I'll see you later."

Marian reluctantly turned back to her desk. It was an amazing creation, built for her as a birthday present by John, which doubled as both a writing desk and a sewing table. The sides were two slabs of black polished marble, each about two inches thick. Across their top was laid another slab of marble, six feet in length, and, half way along and situated towards the front, was an insert of black ash, framing a dark green baize writing surface. This whole block could be removed so that the black, Singer sewing machine, hinged beneath the table on a long wooden arm, could be released and swung into the vacant gap. A black wrought iron frame clung to the underside of the desk, mimicking its shape, and acting as a skeleton to support the ash doors and drawers that completed the front of the utilitarian sculpture.

Marian opened one of the drawers and took out the black stone pen and penholder, which John had also made, and placed them on the table. She looked from these, and then, up and out, through the huge double glazed windows, against which the desk was pressed, and which opened the way for her mind to roam across her rain soaked garden. Looking down at the stone desk again, she suddenly felt that John had got it wrong; the desk wasn't meant to be a sewing table or anything else, it was there purely for the purpose of communication, and now that she had to write a letter that might take a part of John away from her, the only place that seemed fitting for such a letter to be written, was on his table.

Marian picked up the pen and wove it through her fingers. She did not want the stone to go, but she felt as though it was making the choice for her. As her mother had said the stone was dry, but the block of Elm, upon which it stood, was soaking wet and starting to crack. More than this, however, Marian had peered into one of the cracks and felt certain that she had seen a green bud forcing itself out of the supposedly dead timber. What troubled her mind most of all, however, was why she had found herself staring into the cracks of the Elm in the first place.

Ever since she had first found herself clinging to the stone in a faint she had been having troubled dreams. Every night she had felt that she was somewhere else and someone else, but always the same person. Tall and strong, yet helpless, she was strapped to the rock whilst the wind and freezing rain lashed her cringing frame. The elements pounded her body whilst she fought against her bonds, until tired and exhausted she collapsed from the unequal struggle. Each time she had awoken from this cruel and chaotic dream she had found herself huddled around the base of the stone in John's workshop; and, each morning, she had suffered from a terrible headache, almost like a hangover. She had thought that this was due to her lack of sleep, but when she had gone to the doctor, to ask for some sleeping tablets, the doctor who examined her, informed her that she was dehydrated. The doctor had told her that she needed to drink lots of fluids and he wanted to conduct some further tests, to check for diabetes. Marian, however, knew the reason for her troubles: the stone was draining her. If she did not get rid of the stone soon, it would continue to fight against her, and she could guess who would win.

As she finished addressing the envelope to Mr Alexander Balchin, she looked through her selection of stamps and then, for some reason she was not quite sure of, decided to send it second-class. She needed to delay the inevitable; she needed more time.

Theories Examined

Warm air, redolent of the damp grass over which it passed, rolled around the side of the hill and ruffled the pages of the pad next to Jonathan's side, causing him to reconsider his chosen shade of green, before it passed by, hugging the ground, and slipped downwards from the tufted ridge to reach David with whispers of approaching summer, childhood holidays, days gone and days to come.

An exasperated voice lifted David from his reverie, and he turned his attention from the hillside back towards the group of professional and amateur historians who had gathered for their morning meeting.

"All I can say is that the stone has moved," John said, holding his curved hand above his eyes as shelter from the early morning sun. "But how it moved I do not know. There has been too much activity around the site. I know it's not your fault," he said, exposing his eyes in order to hold up a placatory hand to George, "but the site has been damaged by too many feet and one too many explosions."

Balchin was standing with his back to the sun, facing John. The archaeologist's long shadow stretched out towards his companion, but John was stationed beyond its influence, and squinted at his supervisor's silhouette. Emerging from its two dimensional source, Balchin's voice suggested dissatisfaction: "So, even if you can't be certain how it moved, what are the options we have left to consider?"

"Landslide," John said. "But, it would have to be very localized and very sudden. There is a possibility that the unusual weather pattern we have been witnessing, hot sunny days followed by heavy showers, could have had something to do with it. The expansion and contraction of the soil could have loosened the earth around the stone and then its weight carried it down towards the river."

"That sounds reasonable," George commented. "Are there any problems with that theory?"

"Well yes," John replied. "Why, for one thing, did the stone stop where it did? Why didn't it continue down into the river?" he paused to survey the group.

Balchin had a theory "It could..."

"And, secondly," John continued. "Why did the stone start to move at all; when it has been buried in the same location for many hundreds of years, through all manner of weather conditions?"

With regal demeanour, Balchin studied his fingernails, his hand held in a loose fist. The silence became uncomfortable before he asked, "And the other possibilities?"

"The stone could, of course, have been moved manually," John stated.

"Well, perhaps not manually," Balchin corrected. "I believe the dictionary definition of the term refers to: 'By human labour as opposed to mechanically aided'. I do not believe that the stone could have been moved by purely human effort." A smile of sage like beneficence cracked Balchin's features.

"It could have been a number of men," David observed, approaching the others from hill. "As you said yourself it's amazing what a group effort can do."

"I hardly think a group of one hundred teenage boys could enter the village unnoticed," Balchin snapped, replacing the smile with a sneer as he rounded on David, "especially by you.

"No," he continued, turning back to John, "it would have to be a mechanical device, and a very large one at that, to move such a weight. There was no evidence of such a machine being present I presume?"

"No," John replied, casting a sympathetic eye towards David. "No evidence at all.

"The stone was buried to a depth of approximately eighteen inches, and any machine capable of dragging it forward through such a depth of soil would have to be huge. I don't think that even with all the rain we have been having it could wash away the signs of such a monster."

"Could it have been lifted?" Mark asked.

"No. Those are definite drag marks made by the stone: its base is very uneven, you can still see the marks it left, they're even clearer on the photographs that were taken on the first day. That's also the reason why it wasn't pushed over and dragged: it would have left different marks. I just can't see how a stone of that weight could have been dragged upright through the ground," his hands, which had seemed to be weighing up the size of the stone between them, fell limply to his side.

"Any other alternatives?" Balchin asked.

"Just the one," John answered. "It moved itself"

"But the problem is; the stone has no legs," Balchin commented wryly.

"As Sherlock Holmes said," David said smiling from the wall and raising his forefinger in emphasis. "'When all the possibilities have been ruled out, what is left, no matter how improbable, must be the solution'."

"After all," George said, looking towards the river, "the river is said to run, and yet it has no legs; and, as John said, it has moved."

"A very astute observation, Mr Penton," Balchin said, "and to my mind the only one that really matters. The press wish to know how it moved and no doubt their readers are interested in why it moved, but the main purpose of our being here is to research this previously unstudied stone circle and hopefully shed a little more light on the work of our ancestors."

"But the university did also ask us to check out why the stone moved." Mark added.

To David's mind, the discussion seemed to be revolving in ever diminishing circles; he cast a distracted glance over his shoulder and was surprised to find that Jonathan was no longer there. Puzzled, he looked around, and saw Jonathan, bag and drawing board by his side, crouched in the middle of the circle. David pushed himself away from the flaking wall and left the debate behind to join his friend.

"What's the matter?"

Jonathan looked up from where he had been scraping at the ground with his Swiss Army knife. "You know the feeling that I had when I first came here?" he said.

"What, like someone was walking over your grave?" David said.

"Yes. I've just had a similar sensation."

"Is it another stone?"

"I don't think so. I can't see it for one thing, and the feeling isn't quite the same. I'm used to the feeling I get from the stones now. In fact I hardly ever notice it, but this is stronger and somehow has a different tone."

"You can hear it can you?"

Jonathan looked annoyed: "Don't make fun of me. This is real."

"I'm sorry," David apologized. "But you say that you can't find anything?

"Nope, but it's here. I don't know what it is, but it's here." He hit the ground with his clenched fist, and, when he took it away, all that could be seen of the knife was its red handle sticking above the ground.

Ordinary People With Strange Pasts

Michael studied the face in the mirror. Dark, fine, brown hair fell across the brow from a traditional side parting. A far cry from the grunge style it had supported in days gone by; in that lost youth that the eyes seemed to remember with a twinkle, and the lines around them with an addition to their ranks. Good cheekbones, a strong jaw, as a journalist he might even go so far as to say a resolute jaw, but again the lines told their own story. They teamed up with the burgeoning bags under the eyes to show that their origins lay in a riotous past where drinking and laughter took the lion's share of his day. But was it such a long time ago? Chronologically no, but, in lessons learnt, a lifetime. It was indeed a different life he had led only five diaries ago; a life which he had thought his talent would sustain forever. At college, he had been known as one of the best writers ever to pound their keyboards, and he had imagined that each future article would be eagerly snatched up by the world's press.

Enter the real world stage right—steam rolling through his dreams, squashing his aspirations, and putting him in his place. His place was a tiny pinprick on its surface with a label attached saying, 'You are here'.

No longer was talent sufficient. You had to know how to lie, how to cheat and, above all, you had to have the same grasp of human psychology as a double glazing salesman.

Look at that dull, boring, brown raincoat. Look at that stupid conformist haircut. Did they suggest that the wretch they clung to was a self-confident individualist? An anarchist who would write what he liked and the world be damned? No, they insinuated that here is a, 'Mr Ordinary': no one you can take offence to. Tell him your secret troubles, they'll be safe with him—who would take him seriously anyway?

Michael looked at himself and shuddered.

Why had Jane suggested that they meet here anyway; he had asked for a venue where they could talk privately, and she had suggested this hall of mirrors, which was supposed to be a café. Admittedly, the music was loud enough to cut out any chance of being overheard, but there were so many reflections bouncing around that not only could someone read your lips from eight tables away, but you could also see if your earlier contortions had effectively washed the back of your own neck.

However, he did like Jane, and he could see why she had succeeded in a field where he had merely survived. It wasn't just feminine charm, he knew enough of himself to know he wasn't sexist in his views, it was her entire personality. She had no need to don a plebeian uniform: people instinctively felt that here was the confidant they had been waiting for all their lives.

Even the darkest problem, that time had entrenched into their soul, could be unburdened on Jane Appleby. He had felt it himself. It was not as though she was a surrogate priest, far from it, but it seemed as though she had heard enough dark stories not to look shocked, and she did not pass judgement. At least, he guessed, not until she wrote her story, which was when her confessors might realise that they may have made an error in trusting her.

A mantle of red hair entered one part of the kaleidoscope and passed into another and Michael saw six versions of Jane descending upon him, each image subtly different in its perspective. For a moment, Michael's lateral mind connected to the theory of an infinite universe in which there were no limitations to possibility, and, therefore many clones of himself could exist on different planes, each acting out this scenario in slightly different ways. Maybe this was how it would look if they were all seen together.

"That looks nice."

The hand that rested briefly on his shoulder made much more impact on his senses than did the words which accompanied it, and it took a while for Michael to realize that a reply was expected.

"Yes. They seem to make a good cappuccino." Even though the hand had gone, Michael could physically remember the sensation of its light pressure.

"I might try one." Jane brushed the short, light-grey skirt of her suit beneath her as she sat down. "I've only had their coffee before. I might even have an omelette. Are you eating?"

"I certainly hope to. I'm starving."

"Oh. I'm sorry. You shouldn't have waited for me."

"Don't worry, it's no problem, I haven't been waiting long. Anyway," he laughed, "this cappuccino is like a meal in itself; there's so much cream on the top."

Jane smiled in return, and then lifted her head to look towards the waiter. Maybe it was the diamante broach that sparkled as she turned that caused the waiters immediate response, or maybe it was simply that he had not taken his eyes off her since she had entered.

"I'll have a ham omelette please and a cappuccino," Jane said.

"The same for me please," Michael responded to the waiter's raised eyebrow and nodded head.

"So," Jane said, once the waiter had departed. "What is all this cloak and dagger stuff about then? I see you've brought your 'spy raincoat' for the occasion."

Michael merely smiled in response and rested his elbows on the table as he leant towards her. "I've got a story which is very much connected to our stones. About a young hoyden who used to trouble this area, but I can't use it, or, to be more accurate, I'm not going to be allowed to print it. You could, however, and I'm willing to give you the story. The one condition is that you give me joint credit in your paper."

"Why don't you just freelance it out to some other paper?"

"I'd like to do you a favour, I'd like to work with you on a project, and, I think this story would benefit from your touch."

"It sounds interesting, tell me more."

Nunc Dimmitis

The fact that there was only one track leading past the platform gave some indication of the frequency of the trains stopping there. George strolled up and down its length, past the floral pots and hanging baskets, anxiously drumming his fingers against the side of his leg. It was warm and he was feeling uncomfortable. The shirt was sticking to his back and the Harris Tweed jacket did nothing to ease his discomfort; stiff and itchy it cramped his movement. He did not even know why he had worn it; the last time that it had emerged from its hibernation in his cupboard had been when he had taken Linda for a meal at the Hamilton.

The only other person present was an elderly lady, intermittently watching George and reading her book from the sanctuary of her bench. Three cases surrounded her position, effectively laying her claim to the seat and that annoyed George, not because he wanted to sit down, but on principle.

A young porter emerged onto the platform, towing an empty trolley. He opened a doorway at the far end of the building and dragged three bulging mailbags into the daylight. Slipping his shoulder into the middle of the first the porter tried to hoist it onto the trolley, but the bag's bulk proved too much for him and it thudded back to the ground.

George strode over, seeking a diversion from his thoughts. "Can I help?" he asked.

The porter looked up. "No it's okay," he replied. "I think I can manage, thank you."

"It's no trouble really," George assured him.

The porter gave George an appraising look, and believed him. George looked solid. Not the sort of solid used to describe glibly someone who is big and broad, but the sort of solid with which you would never dream of arguing. Given a choice between crashing into a wall and crashing into George, the wall would receive most peoples' attention—walls did not hit back.

In less than a minute, the trolley was loaded and George stood back from his labour as the guard walked onto the platform. "That was quick work Chris," the guard praised. "I was just coming to give you a hand."

"That's right," George said, clapping the young porter on the shoulder. "You've got a good lad here; he shifted all that lot by himself. I was just complementing him on his work."

The blare of a distant horn cut across the platform, and, over the shoulder of the porter, George saw that the train approaching around the bend. He smiled a farewell at the two men and turned to make his way back down the platform—this was to be a private moment.

The train slid into the station as silently and as graciously as a high speed toboggan on cobbles, and clattered to a halt. Its doors were flung open and its brightly coloured occupants disgorged onto the platform, their bags bulging with holiday clothes and rainwear—just in case.

With his mother's amplified height, his father's width and wearing his old pilot Jacket, Harry stood out from his fellow passengers as starkly as a Shire horse amongst a herd of carnival ponies. Heads bowed in their own worlds and conversations the small crowd bustled past him, almost tutting when they found their way blocked, but thinking better of it when they realized the size of the obstacle.

Harry's gaze quickly picked its way through the crowd until it alighted on his father, who merely nodded in greeting from the platform exit. With a returned nod, Harry joined the flow and walked towards his father, grinning.

Even from that distance, George could see the mark left by the cleft lip that his son had been born with all those years ago. His dear Catherine had been so worried that he would be scarred for life and taunted by the other children. George smiled to himself. If only she could see their son now; her legacy to the world. Tall, fair haired, blue eyed and one or two freckles thrown in for good measure; any girl would be proud to be seen with him now, even if there was a slight twist to his lip. It hadn't even seemed to affect him as a child: he had been too big to taunt and no one had dared to try; apart from the one girl.

George's thoughts were prevented from wandering down a particularly nasty road by his son walking up to him and holding out his hand.

"Hello Dad."

George slipped his big hand into the strong but weaker grip of its mirror image and noted the hard skin; his son was working hard. "Hello there, Harry. How are you keeping?"

"Oh, fine. I'm looking after myself."

"I can see that you haven't exactly faded away," George smiled.

"Come on," he continued, taking the bag from his son's hand." Let's get going."

"That's fine by me," his son said jauntily. "And, while we are in the car you can tell me the news, such as it is. Has much been happening?"

"You could say that," George looked down at the bag in his hand, and nervously drew in a breath. "Actually there are one or two things I need to talk to you about, but I think I'd best tell you in the car."

Harry sat rigidly upright in the passenger seat. He had been looking forward to this journey, driving through the countryside he knew so well and reacquainting himself with its pleasures. Now, however, it was all drifting past unappreciated, like a succession of pictures that did not know that they were meant to be a film, blurring past in the visual equivalent of white noise.

"So what you are saying," Harry said turning to his father, "is that you sold the stone, the stone that has been in our family for ever, to raise money for the farm. But, then, when the council said they wanted the field, you moved the other stone to get the attention of the press. You didn't need to do that however, because in the meantime, young Danny Jones had got his legs practically blown off whilst trying to write on the stone that you had moved. So now, we have a team of archaeologists and the press buzzing around the farm, with the occasional visit from a Norwegian helicopter pilot an accountant and a poet-come painter. Not only that, but the general word has gone out in the national press of 'Can we have our stone back please?'."

"That's about it, yes," George said staring ahead and not daring to look at his son.

"Ah. Marvellous!" Harry gritted his teeth.

Entreaty For Help

David took half a slice of toast and slipped it under the fried tomato, so that it matched its companion, and brought his upturned fork down to squash the seeds over the rapidly softening toast.

Many people associate a love and appreciation of food with an artistic temperament, but if they watched David eat, they would know that he worked with plans and figures. He laid his plate out precisely, and methodically sifted through its contents; taking a bite from each serving in turn as he worked from the outside to the centre of his plate. It annoyed the hell out of Jonathan.

"I'm sure we can cope," David said, cutting a slice of bacon and slowly placing it in his mouth.

"Well you might be able to," Jonathan retorted, "but I've never waited on people before, or made beds, or worked behind a bar, and I don't want to start now, especially, when I'm meant to be on holiday."

"You make your own bed don't you? You know how to pour yourself a drink, and you have certainly made me some brilliant meals. And don't you think my mother deserves a holiday too?"

"Yes she does. It is not fair that she has to wait on us. But isn't there some other alternative?"

"No, not really. Aunty Mary has looked after the business before, but she is the one who's ill and my mother wants to visit." He placed another forkful of mushrooms into his mouth. "Come on," he said, swallowing, "it will be fun. Besides we'll have the place to ourselves."

"Apart from the guests."

"Yes, okay, apart from the guests." David looked at his friend, and then past his shoulder to the table behind. Three elderly ladies were sitting there, and he was certain that their normal incessant conversation had dropped so that they could listen better to his. He caught the eye of one of them and, before she could look away, he raised his hand and gave her a quick wave with his fingers. She smiled briefly and looked back to her plate.

Glancing briefly over his shoulder to see with whom his friend was communicating, Jonathan returned his attention to David. "Alright," he said. "I'll give it a go. But we're going to have to clear it with your mother first; she might not want us to look after her business."

"You wouldn't be able to look after the guests by yourselves," Mrs Pengelly said, tying up her apron strings. "It's far too much to expect I'll just have to tell Mary I can't go."

"Mother, I've lived and worked here for years; and if you can run it by yourself, why can't Jonathan and I run it between us?"

"Because there are the books to keep and the supplies to order, you don't know anything about that."

"Well you can tell us before you go. We both run our own businesses. I'm sure you can trust us to run yours for a few days."

"Well, perhaps you're right. I'll show you the books and the ordering this afternoon, and then you can see what you think, and tomorrow, if you're still keen, you can try a dry run at the breakfasts."

"I'm sure we will manage," Jonathan said, with a confidence he didn't feel, "and I'm sure you need have nothing to worry about, Mrs Pengelly."

Her voice cracked into laughter. "I will always have something to worry about, Jonathan, even if I do leave my livelihood in your capable hands. Anyway, I will see you two later; I've got to go to change the beds, unless, of course, you want the practice."

"No, it's alright Mum, we'll start rehearsing tomorrow."

"Yes I thought you might say that." Her rasping laughter faded slowly, as she left the room.

"If your mother really did have an infectious laugh," Jonathan whispered to David, "it would be more deadly than the black plague."

Small Bones And A Can Of Worms

The air was as a misted glass. The sun, from behind its cover of clouds, had failed to burn away the morning dew and the vapour hung heavily in the air—pressing down on the farm and its inhabitants and smudging their outlines like an artist's damp thumb on his charcoaled scene. Moreover, because the blacks and whites of the grazing cows merged into the bright silver grey of the air, they lost their individuality—pulled into a single identity with the farm buildings and their surroundings by the damp grey bridge that linked and enveloped all. It pressed heavily upon the shoulders of the two men and intensified the tension that lay unspoken between them.

Leaning on the seat of the tractor Harry watched as his father grappled with its timing chain. "I don't know why you bother with this old thing," he said. "It should have been scrapped years ago."

"There is no use getting rid of something if it still works," George replied. He rooted through his toolbox for another spanner. "And the reason why it still works is because I do bother with it. Which gives this farm three working machines instead of two."

"But why bother with it now?"

"Because, to my mind, a service in time saves money that's mine."

"Okay," Harry shrugged. "But, if you want my opinion, your time could be better spent by getting in touch with that woman at the planning office and finding out the proper way to stop this road going through."

"Well I've stopped that from happening for the moment haven't I," George grunted as he pulled the chain free.

"Oh yes you've done that alright," Harry said pushing himself away from the seat in exasperation and walking round to face his father over the engine, but you've done it in the most convoluted and dangerous way possible. There is no guarantee that it will stop them permanently."

George was examining the old chain as he pulled it slowly through his hand. "At least it gives us time to gather our forces," he said.

"What? You are mad. You haven't even told them that you object to their proposal yet. All you're doing is giving them time to get their act together, As if they need it. God! They talk about youth being impetuous. You just go out and do the first thing that comes into your head."

"Don't talk to me in that tone of voice young man. I did what I thought was best. I didn't protest against the new road because I didn't want them to suspect that I may have moved the stone myself to stop it going through."

He hefted the chain in his hand and leant over to show his son. "See that," he said, "it's already started to go."

Harry nodded: "Okay, so you were right about that, but I still don't think that you're right about the farm. You're seeing things with too narrow a view. This road isn't going to affect just you. It has to have a beginning and an end, and all the way along it's going to be annoying people in just the same position as you. What about Carmichael? Is it going through his land? You never know, there might be some action committee formed against it. And I'll tell you another thing; if all these people are complaining and you aren't, that might look a bit suspicious."

George picked up the new chain from the newspaper on the ground, and let out a long breath through his nose. "Fair enough," he said, "I can see your point. I'll ring the planning office today."

"No, I'll tell you what, I'll ring them," Harry said, patting the engine cover. "The can of worms you've opened here with your stones is too complicated for me to handle. You deal with that, and I'll ring the planning office and talk to Carmichael and the others."

"Okay if that's what you want to do, you do it, but don't you want to wait around to meet Balchin and his crew? They should be here by now."

"No thanks, some other time maybe." He turned to go. "It looks as though a couple of them might be here now," he said.

George looked round, "Oh no it's not, not really anyway. That's David Pengelly and his friend. You remember David don't you?"

"Err, yes, yes I do." Harry cast a glance over his shoulder. "Look Dad I've got to go. I'll see you later."

George followed his son's disappearing back with bewildered eyes, as David and Jonathan came up behind him.

"Was that Harry?" David asked.

"Yes. I don't think he saw you," George said diplomatically.

"Grown, hasn't he?"

"I suppose he has since you last saw him." he looked at the two men; they seemed to be nervously expectant. "Is there anything I can do for you lads?" he asked.

"Well actually there is George," David replied. "Do you remember when we first came here, that Jonathan found the stones in the circle by sensing their presence?"

"Yes," George said cautiously.

"Well he thinks he's found something else. It's buried in the centre of the circle and he wants to dig it up."

George's mouth opened, prepared for speech, but his voice failed to back it up, and, for want of support, it shut again. The eyebrows, which had risen with the mouth, also came down and continued to sink into a puzzled frown.

"I'm certain there is something there, George," Jonathan put in hurriedly. "And I'd be as careful as possible not to damage your field."

"How much would you want to dig up?" George asked

"Not much," Jonathan said, "about two square feet."

George gave them both a calculating look. "Alright," he said at length, "But you're going to have to check with Balchin first. It might affect his investigations."

"Thanks George. We'll go and ask him now. Where is he?"

"I don't know he hasn't turned up yet. I'm afraid you'll have to wait around."

Alexander Balchin was not in a good mood. The previous day they had found broken pieces of a small animal's vertebrae in a pit near the site of the missing stone. He had been quite excited about the find at first, but when he had cleaned it, that same evening, any thoughts about dating it were vanquished. It was the backbone of a rabbit, probably *Oryctolagus cuniculus*, the common European rabbit, unknown in Britain until introduced by the Normans in the eleventh century. Then, this morning, the tyre of his van punctured.

"You want to dig a hole in the middle of the circle because of a feeling," Balchin said.

"Yes. George said it would be alright with him if it was okay with you," Jonathan said, trying to weather Balchin's patronizing gaze.

"In more than one sense it is rather in the middle of our investigations." The indulgent posture and tone was joined by a tight-lipped smile. "And don't you think that you might need to remove a rather larger area than two square feet? After all this is a field that has been used for agriculture and its soil is bound to have been turned over. Anything that remains buried must, therefore, lie quite deeply and require an extensive excavation to uncover."

"Well we're digging," Mark said.

"Yes we are," Balchin said, with a harder edge to his voice as he turned on the mutineer, "but we are digging near the stones, where the machinery couldn't have reached. Not in the open."

"Well I haven't done much to this field, and neither did my father," George said in a matter of fact tone, rallying as always to the cause of the underdog. "And, as I can't use this field because you're in it I have no objections to letting the lads dig as much as they like. Well," he said, eyeing the two men, "within reason."

"You could try a non-invasive method first," John suggested.

"What's that?" Jonathan asked.

"A metal detector. I've got one in the back of the van. Just have a scan around and see if you come up with anything."

"Sounds a good idea," David said. "Let's give it a go."

Transcendental Journey

The dark determined wind swept down the narrow defile, heavy with rain. Like the Grey God, Odin, it was heedless of all obstacles and careered past or through them with scant regard. This included the human body that stood blackened and rigid like a part of the blasted landscape.

A lull in the wind allowed the black smoke, previously flattened and dispersed, to haltingly hoist its way upwards and place jealous smudges on the flame red hair before it. The wind returned and the hair flickered out towards the smoke, which darted back to earth as though cowed and beaten for its insolence.

Pale long fingers reached up to the broach which closed the woollen cloak and made it fasten tighter, before following its inside line to secure the seal further down. Washed, green eyes, pointed the way to the forest and her goal within, the sister to her immobility.

Where were her companions now? They had all fled; but then this was destined to be a solitary pilgrimage, and a meeting of one to one.

She took a deep breath and started out across the uneven earth. Fallen spears and swords littered the ground around her, and occasionally caught at her feet. It would have been easier and safer to watch the ground, but she did not; it would have been more comfortable to bow her head to the wind, but it was ignored. As heedful of the elements as they were of her she pressed on towards the forest—whose close knit thatch offered the double edged sword of dark shelter and hidden danger.

The ranks of trees divided and conquered the wind as she stepped between their ancient trunks, their leaves and bark, shed over the years, absorbed her footsteps and the heavily perfumed air that they breathed out, she breathed in. As would a revolving stage, the trees had changed the scene instantly and completely.

She felt her way along the passage in the trees that seemed to open up before her—leading the way to her goal. A branch fell, somehow caught her in her midriff, and then became tangled around her ankles. At the same instant, a hand caught her by the shoulder and spun her round, sending her sprawling to the ground. She looked up at her assailant, half expecting to look into a pair of gentle brown eyes. Instead, she saw her mother standing over her, walking stick in hand. Marian's mother did not adhere to the concept of waking sleepwalkers gently.

Onerous Task To Dig Up The Past

Known to David as, 'the weird sisters' the troublesome trio of old ladies were grouped around their commandeered table, presenting an indifferent wall of cold shoulders to the world, but, missing nothing from behind their bastion of pious disapproval. Yet it was upon this table that Jonathan chose to swoop at the beginning of his campaign—determinedly optimistic and tea towel over arm, he made his approach. "Well ladies," he greeted. "What would you like to awaken your appetites with on this fine sunny morning? As always we have a full selection of cereals, but, you could also have a grapefruit, fresh from the Caribbean and crusted over with a delicious layer of unrefined dark Madeira sugar; contrasting the bitter and sharp with a sweet not tart." He smiled down on them.

"What do you mean not a tart?" the whip crack mouth beneath a villainous blue rinse retorted. "Of course it's not a tart, it's a fruit."

"I think," her bespectacled companion said, laying a calming hand on her friend's arm, "that he meant tart, as in a sharp taste."

"But he just said that it was sharp."

Jonathan stood by; arms crossed—his kindly smile, now, almost stapled to his face.

"I think I'll just have cornflakes if you don't mind, dear," the third lady said with an encouraging smile. "Grapefruit always makes me wince a bit."

"I know just what you mean," Jonathan replied with feeling. Goodwill and enthusiasm were evaporating from his shoulders like Eau-de-Cologne in a desert. By the time he moved on to the next table he was a dispirited man: "What would you like to start with?" he sighed. "We have grapefruit or cereal."

Returning to the kitchen Jonathan found that David had already laid out two trays.

"We want another five toasts," Jonathan reported, "three grapefruit and twelve cooked breakfasts, two without fried bread and another two without beans, but extra mushrooms." So saying he picked up one of the trays and disappeared back into the breakfast room.

"It's no use rushing," Mrs Pengelly said from her watch post at the end of the kitchen table. "You can't hurry the guests' breakfasts."

"We don't want to hurry them, mother," David replied, "we're trying to hurry us. We need to get finished here so that we can start on George's field, and, we only have two days before you leave."

"Well, if my going away will be such a bother, I won't go."

"Don't be silly, mother. You deserve a rest. We can do both things; we've worked out a system."

"Alright then, but don't cut any corners with this system of yours, I'll be watching you."

The departing guests had left the usual debris behind them in the breakfast room and Mrs Pengelly surveyed the scene in the company of Jonathan and David.

"What do we have to do now?" Jonathan asked.

"The tables need to be cleared, the tablecloths removed, and the vases and condiments replaced," Mrs Pengelly replied.

Jonathan examined the edge of the nearest tablecloth, running his fingers along its hem: "It seems a bit of a waste of time," he commented, and without further preamble, he stepped backwards, grasped the end of the tablecloth, and quickly snapped it towards him.

Clink, clink, clunk, tinkle—Mrs Pengelly heard it all above her gasp of horror, but saw little. With dread, she peered out from between the fingers that had risen involuntarily to cover her face. To her utmost surprise, everything was still standing intact upon the table, apart from the tablecloth, which, like a matador's cloak, was dangling from Jonathan's hands.

"Where did you learn to do that?" David asked in amazement.

"My 'Boys' book of things to make and do'. I used to practice for hours with plastic cups of water," Jonathan replied, carefully folding the cloth into quarters.

"Don't bother with that," David said, "I'll do the folding you do the pulling. Let's go!"

So, as Mrs Pengelly watched with a mixture of fright and awe, Jonathan and her son walked around the tables—Jonathan pulling away their covers with a ringing cry of: "Ole!" and David catching and folding them with encouraging cheers of: "Yi Ha! Ariba ariba! Hombre hombre!"

All in all, it was definitely not in keeping with the sober, dignified image of the guesthouse that Mrs Pengelly wished to portray to the world. She was, however, too stunned to intervene, and, by the time she had recovered, the dirty cutlery and plates had been removed to the kitchen, the other table furniture left behind, and the dynamic duo moved onwards and upwards to the bedrooms. There it was that she found that the two men had put the second stage of their plan into action. A series of diagrams on how to make up the perfect bed, drawn by David and labelled A to G, were propped up on the chest of drawers, and, with this as reference, David and Jonathan were moving in unison through the steps of their foreshortened alphabet—all in tempo to their harmonious rendition of: "A, you're adorable. B, you're so beautiful..."

It was in disbelief that Mrs Pengelly closed the door on the songsters and returned to the kitchen for a strengthening cup of coffee.

"No she was quite helpful really," Harry said, laying down his biscuit and picking up his mug of tea. "I'm sure she could have been putting her job in jeopardy with some of the things she told me."

"Such as?" His father asked with interest, halting his search for a clean teaspoon.

"Oh, you know; just small things that could help our cause and not theirs."

"Huh, well she never sounded particularly helpful to me," George said. "It must be you she likes."

"I don't think so; we only spoke over the phone. Maybe you didn't give her much of a chance."

"I don't know, maybe you're right," George said, as he sat down beside his son and refilled his mug from the dark brown teapot. "Anyway what are you going to do for the rest of the day?"

"I'm not sure. I was going to try to see Carmichael today; that Miss Mason woman told me, confidentially, that there were already a few protest groups getting in touch with her. I thought that if Carmichael was going to be affected he might want to join one with us. I also asked Miss Mason to send us a detailed map of where the road is going to run, so we can find out who else might want to join. Other than that, I have no plans, so, if you want any help on the farm just let me know. Have you anything that needs doing?"

George gave a small laugh: "Lots, but especially that top field; it needs spraying."

"Okay, I'll do that then; after I've talked to Carmichael."

There was a sharp tap on the window and they looked up to see David waving a ten pence piece at them. George got up to let them in. Harry bit his lip and frowned into his mug.

"Hello Harry. Long time no see," David said, stepping into the room.

"Hi," Harry said standing up to greet his old acquaintance. "Yes it has been a long time. How are you?"

115

"Oh I'm fine. This is my friend, Jonathan Moseley, by the way."

"Pleased to meet you," Harry said, shaking hands.

"So, how's college going?" David asked.

"Quite well; I'm just about to start my final year. It's not as much fun as travelling though."

"I'd heard that you had taken off on a world tour for a few years. Did you find yourself?"

"Who said that I went away to find myself?"

"No one, I just thought that was why most people travelled."

"Did you? Well, contrary to popular belief, you're more likely to find yourself at home: people, generally travel to meet other people." This wasn't said in an unpleasant way, but, nevertheless, there was a sharpness in the tone, which the spectating George failed to understand.

"And how did you find these other people? Apart from with a map." David asked, parrying the turn of phrase before it could be given.

"I found them en masse. But they did help to put my own problems into perspective."

"Well that's good. I'm glad you enjoyed it," David said, lightening the mood as though he had just rung half time. "You'll have to tell us more sometime. Perhaps over a drink?"

"Yes, I'll look forward to it." Harry's smile seemed unsupported by his eyes.

"Great," David returned. "So, George, can we get on with our digging?"

"Digging? What digging?" Harry asked.

"They're just going to dig a bit out of the middle of the circle," George said, sitting down to pull his boots on over his thick woollen socks. "They think that there might be something under it."

"You can't do that," Harry almost shouted.

"Why not?" George said, looking up at his son in surprise.

"Well you just can't." Harry scanned the room as though searching for a reason. "You can't just have anybody coming in and digging up our fields."

"They're not just anybody," George replied standing up and facing his son, "and I don't understand your attitude."

"I don't want to cause any trouble," Jonathan said.

"Don't worry, you're not," George assured. "He's just in a funny mood. Anyway, we can't have you fainting every time you walk across my field can we?"

Jonathan's lips pursed. "I don't believe that I did faint," he replied.

"It's alright lad," George said, walking over to slap him on the back. "Just having you on. Come on let's dig that field," and, leading the way out of the house, he could feel his son's eyes boring into his back.

"No luck with the metal detector then?" he asked as they walked across the yard.

"No not a beep out of it," David replied, "and I'm sure we were using it correctly."

"To be honest I didn't think you would find anything with that," George said, stopping at the door to the tractor shed, "but maybe you'll have better luck digging. The spades are in here, but take whatever you need." He released the lock and let them in."

"What's this, George?" David asked, pointing at a huge iron girder and pulleys that stood in the corner of the shed.

George looked up from gathering the spades and forks and paused: "That? Oh, that's just my old clothes prop for the washing. Anyway, come on: you two should be digging, not talking." He held out the pile of tools.

"I'll tell you one thing, George," David said, looking over his shoulder as they left the shed; "I'm glad I'm just digging your fields and not doing your laundry."

The recent dry weather had hardened the ground, so that, at first, it was difficult trying to dig through the outer crust. In the end they had to loosen up the ground with the forks first and then break it up with the spades.

Almost as annoying as the hard ground was the fact that Alexander Balchin had been correct; two square feet had proved to be far too small a confine for them to work within, and they had had to treble this area as they delved deeper. However, considering their slow start, the two men's excavations were proceeding at a very good rate: the soil had become softer and more peaty and the deeper they went the easier it was to dig. They forged ahead—Jonathan driving himself on with particular gusto. So much so that David had to almost physically haul him out of the pit for lunch, but, it wasn't long before Jonathan was back down in the ground—hacking into moist, almost saturated, black soil. Now, however, just as they had reached about five feet in depth, they hit what seemed to be an unsurpassable problem.

"Damn!" Jonathan cursed from the hole.

"What's the matter?" asked David, looking down upon him.

Jonathan prodded around his feet with the fork but continued to feel the familiar grating of metal on rock. "I've hit a big stone."

"Well can't you get it out?"

"No. It's a really big one. I don't know what to do."

"Just carry on with what you were doing. Try and find an edge and dig down round it."

Tired from his exertions, Jonathan's gaze roamed upwards to see David lying on his stomach and looking down into the pit.

"Do you want me to have a go?" David asked with concern.

"No thanks. I'll keep going for a bit longer," he sighed. He jabbed with his fork into the side of the pit and felt it bite down into the earth. "Hang on!" he called up, "I think I've found the edge." Swinging his weight on the fork, he felt something below him begin to give way, but he could feel that the fork's prongs were beginning to bend. He threw the fork aside and picked up a spade. Tomorrow's blisters were burning through his hands, but he could tell that he was close to his goal, and vicious enthusiasm burnt stronger still within—beating him onwards. With rapid jabs he dug into the side of the pit and down by the side of the stone. "I think I might have got it," he gasped, as he pushed his weight onto the spade and levered out some more earth.

"Hold it!" David shouted down, half rising from his prone position. "What's that?" he asked, precariously leaning over the hole to point out the object with an outstretched arm.

Reluctantly releasing the spade, Jonathan turned to see what his friend was pointing at. It was a small grey object, not a stone, that had been flung out with his last load of earth. He stooped to pick it up—it was cold and soft like an old turd. "Ugh," he cried, quickly dropping it. "I don't know what it is. It isn't a stone, that's for sure. It felt like fungus."

"Pass it up to me and let me have a look," David said.

"I'm not picking that up again," Jonathan cringed. "You come and get it if you want to." He heard an intolerant, "Pah," escape with David's breath.

"Pass it up on the spade then."

Jonathan did as he was bidden, wriggling the spade under the object to hold it up for David's inspection; noticing that David didn't seem to want to pick it up either, as he merely prodded it with his finger on the spade. That seemed to be enough, however, for Jonathan saw his friend suddenly stop his examination and draw back, nervously contemplating both the object on the spade, and his extended index finger.

"What's the matter?" Jonathan asked, lowering the spade and its small burden, back into the pit, where he could again study it.

There was no reply. Jonathan gaze lifted from the pit, and saw David's hand hanging limply over the edge, the index finger still extended as if forgotten.

"What's the matter?" he repeated.

David was squatting on the edge of the pit, his eyes focussed down upon the object. "I think that you have just caused a post phalangeal contusion," he replied in a softly measured tone, "or, in other words; I believe that the object before you is a severed toe. What's more, I'm pretty sure it's human."

News For 'Toe Day'

The Coffee Percolator in the corner ceased to sound like it had Irritable Bowel Syndrome and settled down to a steady hiss, sending out smoke signals laden with coffee vapour. Jane heeded the call and went over to where it sat on the low filing cabinet behind the door. This was effectively her second alarm call of the day. The first one had bellowed from her bedside cabinet and rung the changes in her body to make it leave the delicious security of her bed for the mayhem of the office. Only on weekends would her brain actually put in an appearance, and even then, just long enough to say, 'don't bother'. Fortunately, for her work, the cup of coffee at the office had the same effect on her brain as the first load of uranium into a nuclear power station: the lights came on and the surrounding area became polluted.

Jane knew she should not drink so much, but when she stopped she got headaches and couldn't work. Of course, she knew that she could try to stop whilst on holiday, but then she did not want to ruin her holiday.

Resting her weight on the edge of the filing cabinet, Jane had only managed to take one sip of her caffeine fix, before the door opened inwards and banged into the corner of the cabinet. From her sanctuary, Jane saw an arm reach past the door and throw a pile of envelopes into her 'IN' tray. She watched as the rest of the Post Boy's body came into view—completing his deliveries to the line of still vacant desks. Jane knew she should pop her head round to say hello, but then she might run the risk of experiencing his sickeningly chirpy, 'Don't worry, it might never happen', and it was still too early in the day to slap a cheerful, preventative, smile on her face. She shrank further behind the door and waited until he went and left her in isolation.

A bright red A4 envelope, obviously sent by courier, stood out from the rest of the dun coloured bags of correspondence, and she picked it out. Regretting the fact that she would have to put her mug down to open it, she took a gulp of its contents and set it down, before flicking the paper knife through the envelope. It was from Michael. Jane sat down to read.

'Dear Jane', it began, 'please forgive the rather bright envelope: I hoped that it might catch your attention.

Attached is a draft of my story that will be printed in the Post today. Briefly, it describes how a part of a toe was discovered buried on George's farm yesterday evening, 27 May.

The police have sent the tissue to be analysed and the excavations are proceeding, so they may soon know the identity of the body.

I was merely allowed to report on yesterday's events. It is, therefore, up to you to speculate on the identity of the toe's owner with the information I gave you on Harry Penton.

I have heard that a T.V. news crew is also on its way—this could be big.

Best of luck, and don't forget to mention my name. Michael.'

Jane flung down the manuscript and picked up the telephone; she was going to need pictures and she hoped that Peter was on the other end of his pager.

Earth Works

The phone rang on Michael's desk, just as he was getting up to go for lunch. He considered ignoring it, but, as always, curiosity and worry of a missed opportunity got the better of him. "Hello," he said.

"It's reception here," a crisp lacklustre voice informed him. "There is a Mr Peter Andrews to see you. He says he doesn't have an appointment."

Michael tapped his fingers on the desk. Should he go down and meet Peter and take him to lunch, or should he bring him to the office. It must be to do with the story, so he might need to use the office facilities. "Send him up will you?" Michael asked the receptionist.

A few moments later Peter was standing opposite Michael's desk. "Hi, Michael, how's it going?" he asked.

"Fine, my story on the bone is being printed whilst we speak."

"Yes I know, that's why I'm here. Have you got any pictures for it?"

"Some."

"Great! Have you got any of them finding the bone?"

"Afraid not I wasn't there at the time."

"Damn. I've got some pictures of them digging the site now, but it would better if I had a couple of the discovery itself."

"Do you think your readers would really have wanted to see pictures of a rotting toe being hacked off in their newspaper?"

"I suppose not. Mind you, we do have some funny readers; you should read our Letters page.

"Oh well. Thanks for your help," Peter grunted, picking up his ever present camera bag. "I'd best get this lot back. See you soon."

"Yes, see you, Peter. Oh, by the way, do you know if the T.V. news has been over there yet?"

"Apparently a regional chap turned up," Peter said, stopping at the door, "but there was no camera crew. It's just going to be a news desk item."

"Oh." His tone dropped along with his hopes. "Never mind, I'll see you soon. Bye."

"See you." Peter raised his hand and was gone.

Michael's fingers did a quick paradiddle on the desktop. Should he go for lunch now or try ringing George. Lunch, he decided: it was impossible for him to think or make a decision when he was hungry. Not, he realized, a particularly good quality for a reporter to have, but there wasn't much he could do about it. He wondered if any other journalists were like that.

George came off the phone from speaking to Michael, and, as with Jane earlier, he had had to admit that nothing much had happened in the past twenty hours. At least there had not been many developments that would interest the public, but it felt like a lot had happened to him personally. Not only had Balchin brought in more crew and equipment, but, he had also informed the Home Office of their find, and, as a result, several police officers had also been milling around, much to Harry's obvious discomfort. However, when the inspector had made a brief appearance, the atmosphere became even more charged: especially when he had commented, with a significant look in Harry's direction, that he, too, always liked to see an ancient mystery cleared up. Fortunately, the inspector had left when he realized that there were not going to be many more developments that day.

Indeed, George had been assured, the progress was very slow by comparison to police standards. Of course, they took their time when they were exhuming a body, but they were never as finicky as this. Balchin and his team had not only discarded the spades in favour of miniature trowels and probes, but, they were also carefully sifting each small portion of soil in an attempt to discover what Balchin referred to as, 'historical clues', or, on one occasion, 'fragments of frozen time'. This last had somewhat surprised George, as he did not think of Balchin as being the poetic sort. Obviously, he was not as pragmatic in his approach to his work as he liked people to believe. George could understand that though—he loved farming. If he ever mentioned or hinted at this, however, most people looked at him askance. It did not seem to be the done thing to enjoy your work, and nobody took your views on it seriously if you did. It was as if you weren't being objective enough to judge it with authority.

The telephone rang again, just as George was leaving the house. It wasn't often that he received calls—after all, he was out of the house most of the day, so no one usually tried to contact him until the evening. It seemed to him that nothing of his old routine existed in its original form these days, but what could he do about it? He took off his wellingtons and trudged back to the phone.

It was Miss Mason; she had some information for Harry. George informed her that Harry was working and couldn't be easily reached, so he asked if he could help. When she, very nicely, told him that, as she had been dealing with Harry the information she had would be more pertinent to him; George was more than a little peeved. It was his farm after all, and, although he hoped to eventually pass it on to Harry, he did not intend it to happen for quite some time to come. He, therefore, told her rather curtly that he would get his son to ring her back, and left to start the evening milking.

By the time George had turned the cows back out into the field the light was beginning to fail, and Balchin had told his team to pack up. They were reluctant to leave because today they had uncovered two large, thin, slabs of sandstone, which seemed to cover a pit or grave, and which were now ready to be lifted. It was easy for the team to imagine what they might find under the stones, for the slabs were of an uneven fit, and had left the grey remains of an incomplete human foot projecting into the pit. Unfortunately, it was now too late in the day to expose the rest of the body and arrange the equipment for its preservation, so they covered it with plastic sheeting, to retain its moisture, and gathered their equipment together. Excitement bubbled up in the voices of the team as they prepared to take their leave—their conversation, rather morbidly, centring around their hopes of finding a complete body under the stones. Only one voice was not raised in happy expectation of what tomorrow might bring, and that was Balchin's. Too full of hopes for speech, he left the happy banter to his colleagues, and, instead of retiring to the Crown with the others, he returned to his hotel.

Sleeping Partners

Balchin walked along the still warm road, its soft-tarred stones cushioning his footfalls and drinking in their sound—thirstier than even the long stemmed, rustling, verge.

The warm air leeched the aromatic oils from the wild flowers, which lined the hedgerows, and carried their many varied characters spiralling upwards in a symphony of scent, towards their appreciative audience of one. Even on such a mission as this, where he was afraid of being caught in the midst of his misdemeanour, Balchin could still appreciate, and wonder at, the complex preparations which were involved in nature providing the, so called, simple pleasures of life.

Ever since he had been told as a child to rub a Dock leaf onto a nettle rash, he had been fascinated by nature's remedies, and had made a study of their properties and use. Indeed, he had become something of an old-fashioned medicine man; helping many with his cures. Not that he had any great altruistic drive towards the welfare of others, rather he used them as human guinea pigs, but, if they were cured, they could not very well remain sceptical about his theories. Mark had been a confirmed cynic until his abscess had been cured with a tincture of Broom twigs; and even that fop, David, had to concede that the distillation of Witch Hazel and Arnica had helped his cut hand.

Balchin considered that it was his love of nature, which made him, resent David and Jonathan so much. As far as he was concerned, theirs was a totally unnatural relationship, only made possible by civilization creating an easy path for them, and negating their need to worry about survival or propagation of the species. Not that, Balchin wished to see the likes of David or Jonathan passed down the generations anyway. He pursued his twisted line of reasoning as he stalked along the road, coming to the perverse conclusion that perhaps it was the survival of the fittest that was pushing David and Jonathan out of the gene pool. He liked the idea, and smiled to himself at the thought of the gene pool being cleansed of its mutations and reverting to the purity it had known in pagan days, when people respected nature and lived by its ways: a properly civilized society.

A wavering screech flicked through the heavy air. *Tyto alba.* Balchin looked up from his brooding; searching for the Barn Owl whose scarcely heard call had snatched at his attention. Just in time, he caught sight of its white underside lifting over the roof of the Penton farm, which, luckily, lay in darkness, and so boded well for the safety of his venture.

Balchin leant on the wall and looked around: the coast seemed to be well and truly clear. He placed a foot on the stones and pushed himself up, but, in so doing, a vivid, cold, image of David and Jonathan building this particular portion of wall, flashed into his head. He dropped back to move to another section.

Considering the imposing length of Balchin's gibbon like frame and the fact that fell walking was amongst his favourite pastimes, he made a surprisingly inept attempt at climbing over the low wall. Having placed his first foot too low in the wall's stonework, he was unable to swing his second to the other side. Consequently, he had to take another step up the wall and teetered there for several seconds before he attempted to bestride its top. Even then, he banged his knee and fell sprawling to the ground.

The fact was that creeping around in the night like a thief, made him nervous, and nervousness was a condition virtually unknown to Balchin. Not that he was doing anything illegal, he had told himself; if discovered, he would simply tell the truth, or a modified form of it, but that would reveal a side of his nature, an emotional side, which he would rather remain secret.

Salmon are driven to surmount impossible obstacles in search of their spawning grounds, but, Balchin was driven to look at the body. More than that, he needed to be the first person to see the body: to have a moment alone, a moment of communion with this builder of circles, this messenger from another time—his time.

A reasoned side of Balchin's psyche knew that it might only be part of a body under the slabs, or a more recent corpse, but then another part of him, the driven part—the part he had learnt to trust, knew differently, and he had to resolve those differences.

Climbing quickly to his feet, in the shadow of the wall, Balchin brushed himself down and looked towards the farmhouse—still no signs of life.

Half crouching, he ran towards the standing stone to where, earlier in the evening, he had hidden a crowbar and two spades. They were still there, wrapped in a sack. He picked it up and, still crouching, ran back to the burial site; the tools cradled in his arms. If anyone were watching from a distance they might have believed they were seeing the fabled stork delivering a baby.

Dropping his load, Balchin removed the plastic sheeting and folded it back upon itself in the grass. He looked at the stones. Which one should he lift first? The one exposing the toes looked easier to lift, but, the one that covered the head would probably reveal the most information. He decided on the latter.

The crowbar fitted easily under the slab, and Balchin put his weight against the lever. He swore under his breath; the pivot of the bar had merely sunk into the soft soil. He looked around for something to wedge under the bar. All that lay around him was a field, whose colour deepened into black as it stretched away.

Grabbing hold of one of the spades, he pushed its blade under the bar. Another heave and the slab moved.

Holding the bar down with his foot, he reached for the second spade, forced it into the gap and tried to use it to lever the stone up. It would not work; it was at the wrong angle and it kept slipping. It was also leaving marks that the others would find in the morning.

He released the spade and, still standing on the bar, thought about his next move. He was getting desperate; he couldn't just leave it.

Finally, squatting down, he placed his hands under the stone and, keeping his back as straight as a weight lifter's, heaved his whole body upwards. It was an incredible feat—soil and stone fragments spattered down from the slab, as it was hurled from its bed of centuries by the frantic hidden force in the long, lanky frame, which was Balchin. The momentum of the movement almost carried him forwards into the pit. Only by following the course of the slab and striding over the gap did he stop himself from actually falling in. There he stood, split legged, and standing over the grave like a headstone, looking down on the dank, noisome, time capsule he had hoped to find for so many years.

A heavy, sweet smell of earth and decay rose towards the sky it had been separated from for so many years; but the humid, heavy upper air, held it at bay and would not let it rise far into its thick mass. Maybe that is why Balchin's head swam with mists of visions, caught between the spirits of the earth and the heavens: the half way house between the past, present and future. Or, maybe, it was the fact that here was everything he could have hoped for; the perfect Mercurial runner from history; handpicked to deliver his fraternal message. No circle builder was he; the remnants of robes with the metal clasp that still clung to the curled up form were of a more elaborate design and the rusted remains of the sickle that lay by his shoulder, undoubtedly, pointed out his true identity.

Balchin stood for a moment contemplating the husk of what he knew had once been a living man: eating, drinking and sleeping the same as he, but in a different world. A world where he was a member of the oligarchy that, by virtue of their judicial wisdom, their knowledge of nature and their bardic skills, shaped and ruled the people around them.

This, Balchin thought, would put a spanner in the works of all those who suggested that the druids were tied to their oak forests and had no connection with the stone circles. Here was the dying proof.

The night air was humid enough for the body not to be overly damaged by its exposure, but Balchin knew he should reseal the slab as soon as possible. There was, however, one wish yet to be fulfilled.

Shuffling backwards and detaching large crumbs of soil, which rolled into the hole as he did so, he squatted down at the head of the pit. It went against all his training, he knew he shouldn't do it, but, none-the-less, he reached down towards the finely structured skull and the grey, leathern mask of a face stretching tightly across it to expose the cracked teeth beneath.

A bonding, a shock of realization, a sudden insight into another world? None of these things, which he had half expected, half hoped, happened. Instead, it was as if he had merely touched an old kipper.

He sighed and stood up, ready now to replace the slab, but, as he moved around, something caught his eye. The attitude of the body seemed wrong, lying on its side was unusual enough, but there was something else as well. He crouched down again. There were two bodies in the pit! The one he had touched lay alongside and on top of another. What did it mean?

Flinging himself to the ground, Balchin searched the dark ditch with his eyes. It was no use; the other body was almost totally concealed by the first. He would have to leave it for the others to excavate in the morning, when proper notes could be made of the positions, but what did this mean? Before he fully realized what he was doing, he had reached into the ground, grasped the first body by the shoulder and pulled it out of the way. Thankfully, it did not come apart in his hands, but it might have been better if it had, for what Balchin saw shocked and sickened him to the core.

The second body also appeared to be male, but it looked very small and young: Balchin guessed about twelve years old. Its back was nestled against the adult's body whose arms held the youth between them, but it was the hands that affected Balchin so adversely: they intertwined with each other, as though holding hands on a summer stroll, and the wrists were bound together. Black stains on the bonds, arms and hands could only be blood.

This druid, this originator of his beliefs, this administrator of the laws of nature; went to his death bound together with a young boy in some kind of blood sharing ritual.

Balchin rolled onto his back and looked at the sky. He put his hands over his eyes trying to shut out the image he had just seen, but it did not work. His fingers clawed through his hair. It couldn't be, it couldn't be true, not with such an important find as this; the ramifications would be appalling. The first major news story concerning the ancient druids would portray them, at best, as bloodthirsty barbarians, and at worst as paedophilic, homosexual religious zealots.

What could he do? He couldn't let it happen; but it was the truth. No, it wasn't his mind snapped back. It was just one isolated piece of evidence and it was not representative, but how could he prove that to the media. This was the one concrete piece of evidence that had been found about the early druidic customs; the press were bound to latch on to it as conclusive proof.

It wasn't going to happen: he wasn't going to let it happen. It went against all his archaeological training and the professionalism that he held so dear, but he wasn't going to let it happen. He jumped up and searched for the penknife in his pocket. There it was, a multitude of tools, but all he needed was the blade. He leant into the pit, and, cursing himself constantly for what he was doing, cut the bonds between the two bodies.

Tears of shame, anger, and guilt were in Balchin's eyes as he leant into the pit, and they shook his frame as he moved the adult's arm out of the way to break its union with the boy. Nevertheless, the deed committed, he continued on his dishonourable course with the grim, determination of a surgeon excising a tumour from the healthy flesh of his patient, or, of a vet removing a parasite from its living host. He ripped up the remaining slab; the final cloak of decency, and, dropping the plastic sheet into the hole, and using the blade of a spade to push it between the two figures, managed somehow, with much tugging, prodding and straining, to thread it under the boy and bring it up the other side. All that was left to do was to move the body, and, Balchin knew that this would be the real test of his strength and resolve. Bracing his feet on either side of the ditch, he stretched his arms down, brought the corners of the sheet together, to form a hammock, and pulled with all his might.

If he hadn't been so angry he might not have made it, but then he wouldn't have done it in the first place. He wanted that body out of that burial site, where it should never have been in the first place; and out, it came, leaving behind its home and partner of centuries.

The worst was done; all he had to do now was lay the child to rest once more in a place where he would remain undiscovered. The hedge in the next field seemed the ideal spot: there was no real grass next to it, so the earth would not look disturbed when he dug there, and the tractor or plough was not likely to come right up to its edge. What there were, however, were many roots, which made digging difficult. Fortunately panic at the approaching dawn stepped in to lend a hand, and a shallow grave was soon carved out.

With no ceremony, but with much regret and a great stab of guilt, Balchin rolled the body into its new resting place, and covered it over with soil.

It was now time to reinter the other body. Having replaced the slab it just needed the sheet, but, as the boy's body had left a stain on the plastic,

Balchin ensured that the soiled side was face down over the slab, before he hid the tools and hurried back to his hotel for a shower.

Transient Dreams

Darkness like a warm blanket lay all around. No stars broke its uniformity, no moon, no horizon, and, because there was no depth to the ether, it was easy to imagine that there was no texture; but there was. It could be felt, it lay close and protectively; and, because there was no depth, there was no fear that dark creatures would creep out of the camouflaged distance to pounce upon their unwary victim. Like a protective swathe, it swaddled its ward with warm folds of security that told its inmate he was home.

A tearing, a light, an intrusion. Searing light and unused, well travelled air burst in. Light that tore into the imagination and made it redundant, air that filled the senses and pushed out familiarity and security, and whispered of a bigger world—an unknown and unsafe world.

A heave, a rent, a lift. Travelling upwards, shards of the past falling away and dropping towards the darkened home. A cry that failed to escape into the air, because the air was the enemy, vicious and new, which might turn upon him with tales to shock his naivety.

Rolled, hurt, dragged by fate, the journey into a frightening future continued. Entropy, change, a race into the future, must all occur, but why must it feel so personal, so isolated, so alone?

Rest and respite. Stop the headlong rush, shut out the light, shut out the new; bring back the security of the old, so that the mind can travel to find its own wonders, and not be forced to see the world's own bitter selection.

Darkness welled up towards him once again, offering sanctuary with no scolding recriminations for having left so abruptly. It folded in again, but it was not home, and things whispered to him from the depths of the darkness. These weren't whispers of the future, they were whispers of the past, and the devil you know can be far more terrifying than the devil you don't. Horrified he stretched frantically towards the light that was slipping away.

Danny sat up, looking around to reassure himself of his bedroom's familiarity. He got up and crept over to climb into bed with his father, who instinctively placed a protective arm over him and curled around him.

Old As The Hills

Six pairs of hands reached under the slab and lifted it in unison. Eleven pairs of eyes stood round and watched.

Matthew let out a low whistle of surprise. "It looks like the druids were here then," he said.

"Yes it does seem that way, doesn't it?" Balchin agreed. He glanced up. The sun was still low on the horizon, but it was obviously going to be another very hot day. "Alright," he said, "let's get that other slab up and then we'd better start the sprays. We'll start our investigation of the site as soon as we can be sure it won't dry out."

The stone that covered the feet, like its partner, was lifted cleanly and placed next to the pit.

"I want those sprayed too," Balchin said, looking up at the two volunteers who stood ready with the hosepipes. "They might dry out and crack in this heat, and it will also help us to see if they have been cut or worked in any way. You never know, there might even be an inscription on them."

The two nodded their understanding and waited for Matthew to finish taking his pictures and move his tripod and equipment out of the way. However, theirs was a long wait, because even though Matthew was working as quickly as possible, he had to make an exact note of the position from which each photograph was taken, so that, later, an accurate geographic representation of the find could be recreated from his prints and Mark's measurements. Finally, however, he was finished, and a fine, mist-like spray erupted into the air. The sun's rays stuck the haze, spluttered apart, and a cascading rainbow descended over the pit.

The onlookers crowded around the perimeter of the protective envelope—looking down on the terminal sleeper, and, as they peered through the shimmering, multicoloured veil, the watchers could not help but feel as if they were looking in on a fairy tale. Each of them construed a different history for the wonder they saw before them, but, for Jane, the figure summoned the image of a character from Arthurian legend: a knight, laid to rest with his sword, and waiting to be awakened with a kiss from a pure hearted damsel. However, it would have to be a damsel with a fairly strong stomach to kiss that, she reflected as the spell wore off.

The first to speak was Peter: "Can I take some pictures, Mr Balchin?" he asked.

"Yes of course," Balchin said, looking up from his note taking.

"What about the sprays?" Michael's photographer, asked. "Would it be possible to turn them off, just for a minute? Only it might interfere with the pictures."

Poor innocent, Jane thought. She readied herself for Balchin's snapped retort. Something along the lines of, "Why didn't you take them earlier?" but it didn't happen. Instead, he replied, "Okay, no problem. Besides, it will give us a chance to connect the sprinklers."

Jane noticed that she was not the only one to be surprised by the archaeologist's response—he was obviously in as good a mood as herself, but, probably for different reasons. Hers was born from the exclusivity of her position. For some reason, she could not quite fathom, George had only allowed representatives from hers and Michael's papers to actually report from the site. All the others had been relegated to standing on the roadside, along with the inquisitive public and the 'New Age Travellers' who had been arriving in their vans over the past few days, but Jane knew that theirs wasn't a totally lost cause—Michael had already made arrangements to sell his pictures and story on to the other papers. She couldn't help but admire his entrepreneurial spirit.

One of the two police officers present stepped back from the pit "Well," he said. "It looks like this chap has been dead for too long to concern us anymore. I presume it is a man?"

"It's hard to say," Matthew replied.

"I wouldn't say that," Balchin stated with flat dissent. "As the corpse is wearing druidic dress it is almost certainly male."

"On the other hand," Matthew countered, "the body's stature is small and the amount of decay limited, but enough to obscure the features. Either it could be a well-preserved ancient corpse, or a more recent one dressed in the garb of a druid. In which case the small frame and slight build would point towards it being female."

"Besides which," David put in, "as the ancient Britons placed much more emphasis on the female role in society, isn't it possible that the druids were an equal opportunities employer?"

The word, bridled, leapt into Jane's mind when she saw Balchin react to David's remark, but it wasn't really sufficient to describe the vision of the archaeologist drawing himself up to tower over the young man. Reared, was a much better word. She waited for the downwards rush and the blast of bitter scorn which seemed to be Balchin's trademark. In the same instant, she realized that, yet again, she was holding her breath, in fear or trepidation of this man's reaction. She did not have to hunt around to find the right words to describe how that made her feel, 'pissed off' fitted the bill exactly.

"There's a telephone call for you, Mr Balchin." It was George, coming across the field and ploughing through the charged atmosphere to create a rustle of released tension. "It's a doctor Robinson for you."

The attack did not happen and Balchin's shoulders dropped back into their stoop. "Ah. Right. Thank you Mr Penton," he acknowledged. "Perhaps these will be the results we have been waiting for. If you will all excuse me."

Jane's eyes followed the archaeologist as he ran across the field; little knowing that she was watching a man pursued by the worrying guilt that he may have thwarted a murder investigation. She felt a presence at her shoulder and turned to find Peter holding up a camera, a beaming smile spread across his face.

"What's in here should set the front page alight and put the punters off their breakfast," he said with delight.

"You'd best look after it then," Jane said returning his smile. "It could be your passport to fame."

Matthew brushed past them, unreeling lengths of hosepipe. "Yes, well it will be a damp passport if you don't mind out of the way," he said. "We're about to turn the sprinklers on."

"I'm sorry. We always seem to be in the way don't we?" Jane apologized.

Matthew connected the hoses. "I'm afraid I might have to say, no comment to that, Miss Appleby."

"Don't worry, Mr Reece, it is a phrase I have often heard.

"So tell me, what is the purpose of all this water? Won't it damage your find?"

"On the contrary, it should protect it," he replied. "It's probably the saturated soil down there that has kept it so well preserved. We're just providing a very light spray to increase the relative humidity and prevent it from drying out. No real water will be going onto the find." He turned to signal to the engineer, and an elongated arch of water flared outwards from the lengths of holed piping running along the stands to either side of the pit.

Jane was still baffled. "But how can you study the body if it's raining down on you?" she asked.

"We turn it off. It only needs spraying at intervals."

It was a simple response to a simple question. There was none of the patronizing sarcasm that might be expected from Balchin. Jane decided she liked Matthew, you asked a straight question and you got a straight answer, there was no ego to contend with. She decided to take advantage of Balchin's absence.

"So, do you think that it might be a female druid?" she asked.

"It's only a vague possibility, one of many," he replied. "There are others."

"Ah, but speculation is the name of the game." It was Michael, butting in with his size nine's before she could ask Matthew to elucidate. "Hear of a good fact, print it, and it's the end of the story. Write about possibilities, however, and the story can continue."

"Yes, thank you for that, Michael," Jane responded. "I was ..."

"Well I'll tell you something. I wish we had a few facts about this case." This time it was one of the police officers chipping in. "Then we would know whether to treat this as criminal or historical evidence."

"Quite. I was..."

"Worry no longer." It was Balchin, out of breath and coming up behind them.

Jane clapped her notebook shut in frustration, and turned on the red-faced archaeologist. "And just what is it that we don't have to worry about, may I ask?" she snapped.

"Err... The find... The lab..." he faltered. "The lab has analysed the tissue of the toe we found. It seems that our find, this body, is old; very old." He paused and swept his eyes over the expectant group. "Over one and a half, thousand, years old."

Jane joined in the chorus of surprise, but did not fail to notice that Balchin seemed more relieved than pleased.

"I'd better let headquarters know," the police officer said.

"Apparently the lab has already rung them," Balchin said.

"Oh. Well in that case I'll see if our services are still required around here."

"They are as far as I'm concerned," George said. "I could do with some of your lads stopping that crowd of hippies from coming onto my land. We don't have a chance to get on with anything around here with that lot constantly trying to get in. Harry's up there now." He turned to point towards the farmhouse, only to see Harry advancing rapidly towards them, brandishing a newspaper.

"What are you doing here?" George called. "You're meant to be at the gate."

Harry continued marching towards them. He stopped and glared at Michael and Jane before facing his father. "I pointed out," he said, with barely mastered rage, "that if anyone stepped onto this land, whilst I was away, they were trespassing; and, as such, I would be within my rights to use force to defend my property. Which," he said biting off the word and turning on Jane and Michael, "is something that I might just do to Miss Appleby, and, Mr Thornton."

"Why? What have they done?" George asked, shocked at his son's anger.

"They printed this." Harry thrust the paper into George's hands. "It was brought to my attention when a young woman asked if I was the person who murdered little girls."

"What!" George scanned through the article and, as he did so, his face flushed through, from shocked white to angry red. "You! You two wrote this! Why? Why after I trusted you, after I gave you my story. Why?"

Jane knew what she had to do. She had to keep someone on the inside. "I'm sorry George," she said, slipping her notebook into her pocket, "but it has nothing to do with Michael. It's my paper and my story. Michael only got a mention because I used some of the information from his article: information that has nothing to do with Harry.

"I was merely trying to find out a possible identity for this body and I got the information from another source."

"What source?" Harry snapped.

"I can't tell you I'm afraid," Jane bit her lip. "All I can say is that I am sorry for the upset I've caused, and, of course I will say, in the paper, that this is an ancient corpse, and that there is no possibility of a link between it and you or your family."

"Very big of you, considering that the evidence of today's find all points to that same conclusion anyway," George stormed. "Just get off my land, and don't come back."

"I really am sorry," Jane said, shouldering her bag. "Come on Peter." Head down, she walked away, leaving an uneasy silence behind her.

Matthew picked up his camera and peered through the viewfinder at the figure in the pit. Something didn't look right. He lowered his camera and squinted over its top. "You know," he said, "there's something strange about this."

Balchin turned his attention away from the retreating back of the journalist. "What?" he asked.

"The grave is too big. If it took so much of an effort to dig a hole, such as this, with their limited resources, why did they make it so much wider than they needed? Unless, of course, they buried it with other objects, but I can't see any."

"Maybe they rotted away," Balchin suggested.

"Could be. When we dig deeper we may find out."

Nomad

Another hot withering day was at an end, and Alexander Balchin sat down in his room to reflect on recent events. The previous days had all seemed to be a succession of starts and finishes with no midpoint—each one starting out with hope, as to what it might bring, and madly rushing on towards the disappointment of having to stop the search with the failing light.

He walked over to the tray that lay on the side table with its assortment of teabags, one portion milk cartons, sugar sachets and gleaming stainless steel kettle. Flicking on the kettle's power, Balchin noticed that there was black earth ground under his fingernail and he went through to the en-suite bathroom to wash his hands, but, as the water was running over his hands, he thought better of it, and, still dripping beads of water from his fingers, stripped to climb into the shower. He really felt a need to wash away the cares of the day. Matthew's words had disturbed him more than his colleague could have guessed. Alright, so the adult body had turned out to be male, but what about the other body, the one that only he knew about. That had not been dressed in a druidic robe, it too had a slight, small frame, and it had been dark. It could have been the body of a young woman or girl.

Balchin hung his clothes on the back of the door, leaned into the shower to turn the tap and gauge the temperature, and pulled back the green plastic curtain to climb in.

Rotating slowly, steadily, like a statue in a fountain, he let the water gush over his body. It took him back to seeing the body, lying in the pit, dowsed with water; an empty space between its arms. It had been a boy, Balchin felt certain of it. If it had not, then his actions and his damning conviction of the druid's carnal appetites had been premature and he, himself, was the abomination. Still, would it have been much better to find a young girl tied next to the body? In his own mind, Balchin knew the answer was, 'Yes'.

He turned in the shower and opened his eyes, trying to push such thoughts from his mind with the reality of his surroundings. Through the gap in the curtain, he saw a letter sticking out of the pocket of his jacket, hanging on the back of the door. George had given the letter to him that morning, apologizing for having forgotten about it until then.

Still dripping Balchin stepped out of the shower and quickly dried his hands. He pulled the letter out of his pocket and slipped a pen under its flap. It was from a, Mrs Marian Dally. Balchin read on, and, as he did so the worries and cares of the day were overwhelmed by a slow rising tide of excitement.

There was no telephone number at the top of the letter, so either, Mrs Dally had no telephone, or she was not concerned about receiving a quick reply, but he was. He threw a towel around himself and ran into his room to find the complimentary writing pad, and to put pen to paper.

That same evening, Jane sat on the sofa dozing; the trauma of the day had certainly taken the life out of her. The straight whisky she had poured herself lay, only partly emptied, on the low glass table in front of her.

She curled her legs onto the sofa, her long, white, cotton skirt draping over the paisley pattern of bright yellows and greens as though it were lying on a summer lawn. Her arm rested limply by her side and her head nestled between the corner of the large rounded arm of the sofa and its back. Cradled like this she journeyed into a hazy wood where the bright sun's rays were filtered through the green canopy to form an incomplete jigsaw of light on the forest floor. A narrow path of brown, fragrant, leaf mould, wound its way like a wavering shadow away from her feet towards an unshaded horizon. Cracks of twigs and calls of birds, marked her progress into the bright future, but she was not concerned about her arrival, as the journey seemed so pleasant. She merely followed the path because it was there and because she felt as if she were being called.

One more step and, instead of a bright clearing, she entered a white room. On its floor were white tiles and in its centre was a huge stone. It dominated the room—its dark tones thrown into sharper contrast by the white walls. All but one corner of the room seemed illuminated, and that corner was very dark, as if a section of the wall had been removed to create the entrance to a passageway. The stone's colour was crisp and sharp, but the tall, thin entrance to the tunnel held the blackness of soil: uneven, crumbling, wriggling with worms and insects. Cold, loam scented air billowed from the gap into the warm, summer, room, and with it came a thin fragile voice, stretched out on the current of air: "It doesn't want me," it whispered.

Jane sat up with a start, gasping with fear and desperately sucking in the safe reality of her situation. It was some moments before the dulled drip of whisky dropping onto the carpet alerted her to the spilt glass on the table. On still shaky legs, she went to the kitchen to grab a cloth and quickly wipe down the table, before she made her call. She felt an urgent need to contact Michael: her 'Mole' and only contact with the investigation on George's farm. Having saved Michael's fat from the fire, she felt sure he would be only too happy to give her his full cooperation. The editor had loved their story, and she couldn't stop following it up now. Not when she had such a personal link to it, and certainly not when her sleep was constantly interrupted by dreams of stones that seemed intent on transporting her through time and space like so much hand luggage.

She stopped dialling half way through the number as a sudden thought struck her: previously she couldn't remember ever being able to smell in a dream.

Enfant Terrible

A warm glow of embers parted the darkness, spread across the stone flags and stroked a living burnish into the dark wooden legs of the kitchen table. On seeing such a room a writer of fairy tales might be tempted to overlay images of cheerful mice, chattering and dashing about on their errands, but, in this room, they would have been as out of place as a bingo caller at the Spanish inquisition—for the solitary figure, slumped over the table, banished all cheer from the room and cast a pall of loneliness about him.

Harry sat at the kitchen table, a mug of coffee steaming next to his hand. His index finger traced the swirling pattern of grain that ran along the table's scrubbed surface—his mind following its path in confused loops.

It was a mistake to come back home, or at least it had been a mistake to come back now. If he had returned at a time when things had been quiet he might have been able to blend in better, but, no; his father had to create all this fuss, and now, once more, he was the centre of everyone's thoughts and suspicions. It was also a time when David Pengelly had returned—a friend in many ways, but, also, the one person who might expose his previous misdemeanours to the world.

One day he would inherit the farm, and he wanted it; more than anything else, he wanted it. The idea that he would take over the farm that his family had been working for centuries kept him going. He wanted to be a link in that chain of command which ran through the generations.

Home is where the heart is, so the saying went, but for him it was also where the anguish lay, and that was why he had avoided returning for so many years. Now, however, he needed the farming experience, and, if he had gone anywhere else, his father would have felt rejected. Not only that, but, he had also believed that enough time had passed for peoples' memories to blur, and that now would be a good time to try and slowly integrate himself back into the community. How wrong he had been. Talk about digging up the past. A bitter smile dragged across his lips as he cradled the coffee mug between his hands.

If only his own memory had blurred, he would not be as fractured as he was. He fingered the scar on his neck where the rope had left its mark. Perhaps, too, he would not have attempted suicide those five years ago in Bali. A twisted lip and a twisted neck he thought. If he hadn't been so heavy or if the beam of the bamboo hut hadn't been so weak, his troubles would have ceased. Instead, he ended up lying on the floor with a rope around his neck and a roof strewn all over his body. It was the roof that the natives seemed most concerned about, and it had taken him quite a time to talk his way out of being charged with criminal damage.

He pulled the collar of his shirt closer together; he never wore anything with a low neck in his father's company. It was better that his father never learnt of his suicide attempt, he would only blame himself. Of course, it wasn't his father's fault; Harry knew full well where the responsibility for that lay. It lay with the same person who had systematically ruined his entire life, the same person who had kept sleep from him tonight, as she had on so many other occasions. The same person who had effectively ostracized him from the village community, and the same person who had made it impossible for him to speak to any girl, without him feeling that they were laughing at him or hiding something from him. Oh, his father thought him to be a real man-about-town, but it was all false. All the girlfriends he had told his father about were fictional and all the college parties he was supposed to have attended were make believe. He was a haunted man who kept to his own company, but his father could not know that.

He continued to sit in the darkened room and looked out across the fields to see a beam of light flicker across the darkness. It was too weak and in the wrong position to be a car's headlights, it must be someone in the field.

Harry looked at his watch, the luminous dial wasn't glowing, but the firelight was sufficient to reveal that the time was a quarter past one.

If someone were traipsing across their fields in the dead of night, it must be someone up to no good—probably one of those travellers trying to set up camp.

He got up and opened the kitchen door to the yard slowly and carefully, latching it behind him so that it would not bang in the wind.

Keeping low, he crept towards the wall and looked over. The light was coming from the next field past the river, occasionally flickering and illuminating the trees.

Not wanting to risk the gate clanging, he jumped over the wall and ran along its edge until he came against the wall that ran beside the river. He peered over its top. There, just a few yards away and leaning her back against the stone, was Jane Appleby.

Fury and surprise propelled him to his feet and from his cover. "What the hell are you doing here?" he bawled.

She looked around, startled, pushing herself from the stone. "I, err..." Her face coloured with embarrassment. "I was just going for a late night drive. I found myself in the area and so I came to see the stones for one last time."

Harry snorted in disbelief, "You just popped in to say goodbye, did you? It's one hell of a long drive for a courtesy call isn't it?" He jumped over the wall to stand, arms crossed, on the riverbank. "Beside's which," he said, menace replacing ridicule, "don't you remember being told never to set foot on our property ever again?"

Jane looked at her shoes and then, seemingly steeling herself, she straightened to match her antagonist's stare. "I'm sorry," she sighed. "I know it seems as though I must be on a personal mission to make your life difficult, but it's not the case. I took care not to mention your name in my article about the missing girl. I didn't even allude to it, or the identity of your friends and the girl. I merely said that a young girl had gone missing from this area after playing in a game of ritual sacrifice."

"Yes, on this farm. You mentioned that didn't you? Well thank you very much," Harry spat with vicious sarcasm. "Don't you think everyone in this village knows that I was incriminated in the investigation? They might well have forgotten much about it, but now, as soon as I return, there's the past, raked up by you, and spread all over their morning's paper."

Jane looked genuinely guilt ridden. She tilted her head back to the sky and closed her eyes. Seeking for divine inspiration or for a better lie? "I didn't think it would cause you so much personal grief." She lowered her head and opened her lids on eyes of unwavering sincerity. "You were never accused of anything, only suspected; and I thought, that as the village already knew of the story, it wouldn't be telling them anything new." She paused and took in a deep breath. "It was a good news story, and it added depth and human interest to what, otherwise, could have been a boring historical investigation."

"I'm so glad. I hope you received your thirty pieces of silver. But, I can't believe that even you could be so stupid as to believe that what you printed wouldn't cause me 'personal grief'." He glared at Jane, only to see her jaw tighten; and, was that a tear welling up in the corner of her eye? No, it couldn't be possible. He looked away feeling embarrassed, but still, fuming. Turning his back on her, he walked towards the wall. "So," he said, amplifying his voice to camouflage any feeling, "is that why you are here? Snooping around some more, in the course of your investigations? "

"No, it isn't. If I told you the real reason you wouldn't believe me."

"I don't believe you now," he snarled. "Try me."

"I dream about the stone, this stone," she said flatly. "It sounds stupid, I know, but every night I dream about this stone. In different places, in different times, but this stone is always there. They're not even particularly frightening dreams, just very disturbing. I'm being haunted by the damn thing. I know it sounds stupid, I know it sounds hysterical, but you don't know what it's like to be afraid of sleep."

Yet again, she had managed to misjudge him. "You never know, I might," he replied in softer tones. "I still don't know why you are here though."

"I'm here because..." she faltered looking for inspiration. "I don't know why I'm here," she finished lamely. "I suppose it's because in the dreams I seem to be called towards the stone. It's like a migratory urge. When I'm actually here the pressure seems to go away, but then it only appears to fuel the later dreams." She bit her lip and hung her head.

Harry could sense her conflict. A woman who normally dealt in hard facts, and prided herself on being in total self control, a fighter and a winner in a male dominated world, having to confess to being a victim of her own emotions, but he also knew the strength of her stress. He knew what it was like to be pursued through dreams by a nightmare that would not go away, and which had its roots in the real world. He had run around the earth in an attempt to escape his past and his dreams. If his distance from home had managed to dilute the impact of these images from his subconscious, it would have been worthwhile; but it hadn't. He could understand Jane running away from sleep and its terrors, trying, as she said, to ease their pressure. He could understand and he could sympathise; he almost felt as though a common bond had formed between them.

The two protagonists looked at the river that formed the 'no man's land' between them, and the silence deepened. At last Harry stretched across with an 'olive branch'.

"Do you want a cup of coffee?" he asked. "I can't sleep either and I've been drinking the stuff all night. Father's asleep, so you've no worries there."

Jane looked up, and considered him for a moment. She gave a soft smile. "Yes, thank you, that would be very welcome."

A deep silence tried to push its way between the large gap that separated the two walkers, as they made their way back towards the farm, but Jane would not let it settle. She kept making light forays into its depths with questions about the crops and the wildlife around the farm: nothing that might make Harry think she was asking questions as a reporter. She was grateful to him for not having ridiculed her story. Many people would just have laughed at her, but he hadn't. She sensed a kindred spirit and she wanted to befriend it.

The two of them sat and talked all night, there were many silences, but they were easy companionable ones. Jane's confession had been something of a cathartic experience for her, and she felt much easier about talking about other details of her personal life. Harry could sense this, and responded by opening a slit in his Pandora's box of emotions.

When George came downstairs, at five o'clock, it was into a kitchen filled with the scents of Harry cooking breakfast and the sounds of happy chattering. Of course he was surprised to find Jane there, but, he did nothing to dispel Harry's faith in him. His son seemed happy, and that was all that mattered. He merely politely enquired as to what had brought Jane back to the farm, and, when Harry replied for her, that she had come back to apologize, George accepted that as the end of the matter. He knew something pretty magical must have happened in the kitchen last night, but, he did not know what, and he was not going to ruin it by pushing for an answer.

By the time Jane left, two people had new resolutions, and three went on their way with lighter spirits.

Strategic Planning

Jane took a gulp of her coffee and picked up the phone. Stage one, she thought.

It took some time to get through to Snorri Hákon at the air base, but when he finally came to the phone, he sounded as though he were pleased to hear her voice, and, more importantly from her point of view, he was happy to help her out. She knew that there were plenty of helicopters in Cornwall, the skies from the Lizard to St Just seemed to be as littered with them as the land was with standing stones and the cafes were with pasties, she just didn't know if any of them were for hire. Snorri did.

During her conversation with Harry the previous evening, the young farmer had told Jane that the only ambitions he had ever had, apart from farming, were to pilot a helicopter and to be a photographer. If everything went according to plan, the next day should see him sitting in a helicopter, piloted by Snorri, and taking aerial photographs of his own farm. All supplied courtesy of herself. She did not know quite what her reasons were for doing this, it wasn't just an apology, but she did know that it would make him happy, and that was important to her. She had made him unhappy with her story and yesterday she had been responsible for kindling a spark of gaiety within him, but, did she have the power to turn it into a flame?

She dialled again. Stage two.

"Cornish Recorder," the voice from the receiver responded.

"Could I speak to Michael Thornton, please? It's Jane Appleby." There was a pause, an excerpt of Ravel's Bolero, and then another voice spoke to her. "Hi Jane, how's it going?"

"On the whole, not too badly, but I'm afraid that our writing partnership has to come to an end."

"What! Why?"

"For various reasons, I'm afraid, but, mainly because I don't want to write about it anymore. It seems to be upsetting more people than just your editor." She could sense Michael's protest rising. She rushed on. "Also, having heard my doubts, my own editor isn't interested in running the story anymore. As far as he is concerned, now that the body has been exhumed, and it isn't that of the murdered girl, the story is finished, at least until they find out a lot more about the body or discover the missing stone. Whatever the case, he doesn't see it as being headline news again." Jane let the information sink in before she continued. "I think, however, that I've persuaded him to print one more story. It's a story that won't hurt anyone and may even help George Penton."

"What is it?" Michael asked.

"Before I tell you I must warn you that I won't be able to help much: I've got to supervise a photo shoot tomorrow. Will you be free to do the research?"

"As long as it's connected with the Penton farm find, yes."

"I know that all the sightseers to Stonehenge are damaging the site; in fact it's becoming quite a big issue. It also looks as though the large number of visitors to the Penton farm are in danger of damaging his property as well. I thought we could run an article on the harm that is being done to our national heritage by the volume of visitors, and what measures can be taken to prevent it. I can't imagine it will make the front page, but it is something."

"Do you think you can sell that idea?"

"I've practically done it," Jane replied.

"I'll have to do it from a local angle though."

"Well do it from a local and a national angle. You have enough historic sites around you, including about twenty stone circles, to make it work."

"Perhaps you're right. I'll give it a go," he sounded a little despondent.

"So," he continued after a moment's silence, "is there a chance that we might write together again?"

"I certainly hope so; I enjoyed it, and I think we worked together well." Jane responded brightly.

"Good!" Michael's mood seemed to have lifted slightly. "But, tell me, why do you feel guilty about upsetting these particular people? I mean, nice as they are, and I can see your point, isn't it part of a journalist's lot that they always upset someone?"

"I suppose so, but these are just very nice people, and, I must say, I feel guilty about what I've done."

"You haven't fallen prey to old George's charms have you?" Michael laughed.

"No, I was more concerned about his son." The words fell from her lips before she could bite her tongue.

"What!" Michael spluttered. "Not that psycho? You can't be serious?"

"I am serious. I merely understand that he has gone through a lot of problems and I don't want to be responsible for adding to them.

"Now, if you will excuse me, I have a call on my other line, but I'll ring you tomorrow. Bye." Jane dropped the receiver and leant back in her chair, trying to collect her thoughts. At least Michael should now be away from the farm when she went to collect Harry.

Time presses on she thought, time to stop her reverie, time for stage three: conning her editor. After which she would hopefully have time to drive down to Halliggye fogou—the stone tunnel set within an Iron Age village, where, according to Harry, women in particular, were meant to be privy to strange visions.

She got up and walked towards her editor's office. She had to tell him that she was going to the farm tomorrow to check up on the proceedings.

Only when she returned would she tell him that she had been banned from the farm and, instead of reporting to the office, had used her time to do research for an article entitled 'The Destruction of Our National Heritage.'

True Confessions

There was no doubt that the dark oak lent a certain sobriety to the small room. Perhaps it was for this reason that Mrs Pengelly had elected to retain the room's original panelling whilst converting it into the 'residents only' bar. Like a gentleman's club its almost cloister like character imposed a restraint on those who might wish to take anything more than one or two post prandial drinks.

As he polished the glasses, Jonathan looked over the tea towel at his one and only customer: an elderly and garrulous gentleman whose whisky slowly disappeared in fleeting, lubricating sips.

Contemplating his customer Jonathan was beginning to realize the hidden implications behind the phrase 'a captive audience'. Listening passively to this man's barrage of bigoted, self-indulgent opinions on the health of the nation, would have been good training for smiling sweetly at the Gestapo whilst they turned the thumbscrews or stone walling interrogation. David bursting onto the scene like a fox hunt at a funeral was, therefore, a welcome relief.

"Balchin's on the T.V.," David called, skidding to a halt.

Jonathan's startled thoughts came out of their stupor. "What?" he said looking up, but his friend had already departed at speed.

"Excuse me," Jonathan apologized to his customer. "Commercial break," and, throwing down his tea towel, hurried towards the lounge, but stopped before he arrived and raced back to find the elderly man leaning over the bar to investigate its business side. Jonathan brought the steel shutter rattling down. "Beware the guillotine!" he called, as the man's head darted back to safety. "Almost had you there," he laughed, and, with a wink and a smile, he was gone.

The television lounge was reasonably full. All the armchairs were occupied and David was sitting on the sofa nestled between two of the tea sipping 'weird sisters' who had troubled Jonathan at breakfast. David nudged one of them in the ribs with his elbow. "I know him," he said.

"He looks quite dashing," the lady remarked. "A bit like Basil Rathbone."

David looked at her in surprise. "I wouldn't..."

"Tut. Shush," Jonathan hissed, turning up the television and retreating to his position behind the sofa.

"We can gain a lot of information from a find such as this," Balchin was saying. He was pictured against a carefully placed backdrop of the standing stone. "From a study of the body we may, for instance, discover the composition of its community, its diet, diseases and mortality. Whilst from a study of the objects buried with the corpse, we may learn about the dead person's wealth, social status, occupation, religious beliefs and ethnic affiliations."

"Have you found anything definite about this find yet?" the reporter asked.

"From the metallic objects found with the corpse, and its robes we believe that it was probably a high ranking Druid. The tests which have been carried out on a tissue sample, also suggest that it dates from about the time of the Druids."

"I believe that the tissue is remarkably well preserved. Why is that, do you think?"

"Most probably because the soil is very moist around here. Our engineer thinks that one or more underground streams may run to the river through the area."

"Have you found anything else yet?"

"Actually we have just discovered part of an antler, near the stone circle. It could have been used as a tool, and we may be able to date it."

"Let's hope so, I wish you luck." The interviewer said, turning to the camera and returning the audience to the studio.

"Ha!" David exclaimed.

From his position by the door, Jonathan saw two permed heads rocket above the line of the sofa back in alarm and descend to the accompaniment of rattling saucers and tinkling spoons.

"Now that should be interesting!" David went on.

"What should?" quavered the one who appeared not to have swallowed her teeth in fright.

"The dating of the antler." David explained. "It might show us how old the circle is, and, if it does, I bet it's a damn sight older than that Druid lying in the middle of it.

"And I'll tell you another thing," he added, standing up to point an emphasizing finger at his startled inquisitor. "If the builders of that circle knew that their gathering place had been used by a religion as bloodthirsty as the Druids, I bet they would be pretty upset about it," and, so saying, he swept out of the room.

The others watched his departure in silence.

"As blood thirsty as what? What did they do?" David's victim whispered to Jonathan.

"Believe me you don't want to know," Jonathan replied, "and if he volunteers to tell you a story, refuse the offer. You'll thank me for it in the long run."

That evening, after most of the residents were in bed, and the bar was officially closed, Jonathan poured out two bottled beers and went with David to sit in the two large armchairs that overlooked the garden.

They drank in silence for a while, watching a rabbit that was unwittingly browsing on the short grass. It came a little too close, and the heat sensitive spotlights were activated to illuminate the astonished animal, like a magician's prop, centre stage. Transfixed it sat there until Jonathan tapped the French Window with his foot, and it span around and took off into the bushes.

The two men chuckled in unison as the rabbit executed its own vanishing trick and the light switched itself off, signifying the end of the performance.

Jonathan broke abruptly into their laughter, with a question: "Why don't you and Harry get on?" he asked.

David's chuckles slowly subsided. "Why do you ask?" he said.

"Because," Jonathan said carefully, resting his glass lightly on the chair arm, "it struck me that no matter what petty jealousies children harbour against each other when they are at school, when they leave, such things are normally forgotten. They are merely bound together by the common connection of having studied together. Harry and you, however, don't seem to have forgotten your differences."

"And what would you deduce from that my dear Sherlock?" David asked.

"I don't know. That's why I'm asking you."

"He's afraid of me," David said bluntly, draining his glass.

"Why?" Jonathan asked, as his friend got up.

David did not reply at first. Instead, he reached behind the bar and came back with another two bottles. Crossing his legs, he placed the crown cap against his shoe's heel, smacked the flat of his hand on its top and sent the cap spinning across the floor. This was another of David's little acts that annoyed Jonathan intensely, and he felt that David had done it for precisely that purpose.

David settled back into his chair. "When we were boys," he said, pouring his beer into the glass, "at the time when Harry was under suspicion by the police, one of Harry's friends, who thought he was a big man because he associated with a suspected murderer, decided to make my life difficult. He kept calling me names and pushing me around, until, in the end, I hit him—very hard. He then went to Harry and asked him to sort me out, but I told Harry that I had seen him and Sarah Nancarrow, from the hill, playing near the stones. I also told him, that if he ever touched me I would tell the police. I played it very well: I intimated that I knew a lot more than I did, and could tell the police much more than he had. I'm not sure if there was anything more to tell, but it certainly did the trick: he took me under his protective wing, I became one of the 'in crowd', and, eventually, we became friends. I even went to the farm for tea on a couple of occasions, but he never really trusted me, and he always resented the power I had over him."

"You blackmailed him then!" Jonathan exclaimed, sitting upright in his chair, shocked by his friend's revelation.

"Certainly not," David retorted, responding similarly to his friend's remark. "All that I asked for was not to be beaten up, which I've never thought to be an unreasonable request. What was freely offered, on the other hand, was membership to the group. I had merely implied possibilities when he pressed me for answers." David took another sip of his drink, and let his head sink backwards into the padded headrest.

"In my defence," he said languidly, staring at the ceiling whilst recollecting the past, "I did promise him, thereafter, that I would never tell the police. Perhaps he didn't believe me, or suspected that I might tell someone else."

"Which you did."

"Michael Thornton? Yes, I did."

"Why?"

David considered for a moment. "To assuage my guilt. You see I've never really trusted Harry, and I know that there's a black, tormented streak running right through him."

Jonathan knew there was no answer to be made—he had seen the same thing within Harry as David had, so the two simply sat in silence until Jonathan finished his drink and went to wash his glass. "What are we meant to be doing tomorrow?" he asked.

"Visiting Danny Jones, for one thing," David replied. "I promised my mother that we would go over and see him. Besides which I would like to know how he is myself. I saw Mrs Jones yesterday, and she said that, apart from still finding it difficult to move, he's being plagued by bad dreams."

"Poor chap," Jonathan said. "Perhaps we should take him out somewhere. Where do you think he might want to go?"

"Anywhere, apart from the Penton farm, I would imagine," David said, rinsing out his glass and turning off the light.

Overseers

The helicopter rhythmically clawed great chunks of air out of the sky and flung them downwards; pulling itself upwards in the process and producing a staccato boom within its cosy, if cramped, cabin.

Harry was loving every moment of it. He had initially been afraid to lean out of the doors, but now he felt secure within his harness and was constantly taking pictures as they hedge hopped across the countryside. It reminded him of the ski lifts he had been on in the Alps.

Snorri's voice crackled into Harry's headset. "Here's your home, Harry," it said.

Harry looked. The hill stretched up on their right and the farmhouse lay straight in front of them, but, looking over his shoulder, he could also see his father sitting on the tractor making his way across the hay field.

"Let's go and say hello to Dad," Harry said pointing. Snorri nodded and they came up behind the tractor with Harry leaning out of the door.

George heard their approach and turned around in his seat to smile and wave, as Harry took a few photographs to mark the occasion, but, after giving them a mock salute, George peered over the side of his tractor and pointed to the ground. Their down draught was flattening the grass stems, and George was now making shooing motions at them with his hands. They laughed guiltily as the helicopter climbed out of harm's way.

"I do like your father," Jane said.

"Yes. So do I," Harry said. "He has his faults, but he's one of the best."

"Are you enjoying this?" Snorri asked.

"Are you kidding?" Harry said. "This is brilliant. You must enjoy your job so much."

"I do. Everything looks so different from up here. All those tracks running through your fields, it makes them look like those things that were in the paper. What do you call them?"

"I don't know," Jane said, "there are lots of things in our paper.

"You know," Snorri persisted. "Those patterns."

"Oh you mean the crop circles. Yes I suppose they do."

"Can we climb up and get a better overall picture?" Harry asked.

"Certainly."

They traversed the farm, looking at the patterns created by the comings and goings of the people on the farm. The area around the stones was particularly rich in these, but, to Harry's proprietorial eye, one looked out of place. Wide and straight, but broken, it went from the edge of the stones and part way across the field on its left, where the cows were grazing. Since the stones had been investigated, however, this route had not been used; access to the cows was gained through the yard.

Harry asked if they could go down a little lower to look at it more closely. It looked as though a heavy object had been dragged away from the stones; the grass was flattened in only one direction, and had been taken into the other field, where the, broken trail stopped at a small flattened mound. Harry made a mental note to investigate it later.

Now It's Official

The heavy slap which denotes, predominantly, junk mail falling onto the floor, called Marian through from the drawing room. She sifted quickly through the envelopes, until she found one that caught her attention. The dark blue ink and the copper plate handwriting would suggest that it came from John's grandmother, but the postmark did not. She went through into the kitchen and isolated the crisp white envelope in the centre of the table facing her chair. Teapot, cup, saucer, milk jug, knife, ashtray, cigarettes, matches, all were brought and arranged in a protective semicircle about her position on the table. The tea was poured and the cigarette lit—the twenty fourth she had smoked in her life and the fourteenth since John's death. Prepared, she lifted the envelope into her arena and slipped the knife through its flap.

Many were the feelings, which had coursed through her body during the previous few weeks. Some were emotions, created by her own anxieties, others images and sensations which felt so alien and violating that they could have been impregnated into her body by an external entity; but, this was the first time that relief had seeped through her frame, and it felt very welcome.

The letter was, indeed, from Alexander Balchin, and it confirmed what she already knew from the picture in the paper: her stone and that which had gone missing from the Penton farm, were one and the same. John had acquired his stone on the same day that the one from the farm was removed.

Marian slumped onto the table, her head falling into the crook of her arm as she scattered her defences about her.

Initially she hadn't wanted to let John's stone go, because it had felt as if it were a part of him, but, now, she feared that she was becoming a part of it. It had invaded her head in much the same way as it had her home—and both were beginning to crack under the strain. Afraid of sleeping, afraid of dreaming, afraid of awaking in a reality not hers, if the status quo were not restored with the removal of the stone she knew her final resting place would be the psychiatrist's couch.

Obviously, the next step was to return the stone to its original site, but how? She vaguely remembered the name 'Henry's Haulage' being on the side of the lorry that delivered the stone. Maybe, he might take it back again, the number could be in John's address book. She would also ring Mr Balchin to arrange a time of delivery, but, one thing was for certain; when the stone went back, she was going with it.

She heard the click of the door and the scrabble of claws on tiles. Too late were her reactions. Before she could defend herself Bess's wet nose was firmly planted up her skirt.

By the time her mother and Alfred Dart entered it was to the sound of Marian's laughter and to the sight of her wrestling with Bess on the floor, who, rolling on her back, panted doggy breath over her attacker.

"You seem to be better," Alfred commented.

"At least the dark rings under your eyes, seem a little lighter," her mother acceded."

"Well I've had some news," Marian said, releasing Bess and climbing to her feet. "It seems as though my stone is the one reported missing in the papers, and they would like it back."

"And have you seen sense?" her mother asked.

"If you mean, am I going to send it back? The answer is yes; and I'm going to accompany it."

"Wonderful," her mother said. "We can make it into an outing. You never know, Alfred," she said turning to him and nudging him in the ribs, "we may be on the television."

Exhumation

"I'd be glad if you would speak to Danny," Mrs. Jones was saying. "He could certainly do with being taken out of himself."

"Well we thought we might ask him if he wants to go for a walk," David said. "How are his legs now?"

"Well that's the peculiar thing. He says he can't stand on them, and he seems to be in genuine agony every time he tries," she cast an anxious glance up the stairs. "Yet despite that he manages to walk across to his father's bed every night and climb in with him. Not that he can remember doing it mind you." Mrs. Jones stopped toying with the strings of her apron for a moment and Jonathan noticed that the lines of worry around her eyes were beginning to take on an etched permanence. Obviously, her son's illness was affecting her almost as much as it was Danny himself. There was no doubt that Danny's disability seemed much more pronounced and unjust because he was so young and previously so active.

"He even seems to be having trouble with his arms now; his wrists are hurting him and he says it is worse when he moves his hands."

"That doesn't sound too good," Jonathan said. "What do the doctors think it is?"

"They think it must be largely psychosomatic, because, they say if he can walk in his sleep his bones and muscles must be a lot stronger than they seem, but, they still have no idea what the marks on his wrists are from."

"Oh dear," Jonathan sympathized. "What about physiotherapy? Would that help, do you think?"

"Doctor O'Brien has arranged some sessions, but Danny doesn't really want to go."

"Maybe an outing will do him some good then," David said. "It might make him want to get up and about again. Could we take him in the car?"

"Yes I should think so," Mrs Jones replied, a little more brightly. "He's got a wheelchair as well, if you can fit it in."

"I should think we could manage that," David said. "We thought we might take him to Mousehole, to see the bird hospital, or, possibly, to that abomination they've made of Land's End, where they've got some sort of exhibition on."

"I'm sure he'd like either of those."

"Okay," Jonathan said. "Let's go and see what our main man thinks shall we?"

Twenty minutes later the three of them were sitting in the car and, much to Jonathan and David's surprise, heading to George Penton's farm.

"Are you sure you want to go there?" David asked, yet again.

"Yes," Danny replied, "I think I'd feel better there."

There didn't seem to be much room for argument: Danny was the one who probably knew the most about his illness, and so here they were, once more entering the grounds of George's farm and passing the policeman who was there to keep out unwelcome visitors.

The wheel chair came out of the boot much more easily than it had gone in, but it still managed to trap Jonathan's finger in its hinges as he unfolded it.

"Damn," he cursed. "I hate inanimate objects that fight back."

They wheeled Danny tentatively through into the field where the stone circle lay, unsure about what Balchin's reaction would be towards the boy who had tried to vandalise his precious stone.

As they entered the field, Harry was driving into the yard. He was feeling very good about the world at the moment; the helicopter ride had been a fantastic experience, and the lunch afterwards with Jane had also been a great success. There had been so much to talk about during the meal that he hadn't even felt uncomfortable, which was a first for him. With the exception of his mother, he had never sat alone at a dinner table with a woman before, and, on the few occasions he had been in a mixed group, he had always found his conversation stilted and punctuated with embarrassed silences. This had been different, the talk had flowed and the time passed in a blur. More importantly, he had found a woman, and a beautiful woman at that, with whom he felt at ease, and who, he thought, felt the same about him: she actually seemed to like him for himself, with no hidden strings attached.

In short, Harry was a happy man, and the only thing that intruded on his merry thoughts was the worry that someone might have buried a carcass on their land.

Since B.S.E. and Foot and Mouth had hit the headlines, the Knacker was no longer inclined to give money for a carcass, but, more often, asked for money to take it away. This being the case it was more economical to bury the carcass yourself, but burying an animal on ground that other cows grazed was just asking for trouble. His father couldn't have been so stupid, could he? Well he would soon find out.

When Harry found his father and asked him about the trail and the dug earth, George seemed as surprised and as intrigued as he, but he couldn't break off from what he was doing, so Harry, alone, went to fetch a spade and investigate.

David intercepted him on his return from the shed.

"Hello, Harry," David said, as he approached. "Doing a few excavations of your own?"

"Oh, hello, David," Harry said, stopping and hefting the spade in his hand. "Yes, I am. Nothing on such a grand scale as Balchin's team I'm afraid, but it's likely to be a lot quicker."

"I'll get a spade and help you if you like," David said, "Jonathan's taken Danny over to see the Balchin's crew."

Harry considered David. Was this the friend he had known or the enemy he suspected? Perhaps he had misjudged him, perhaps he should have trusted his integrity, and perhaps he shouldn't ruin a good day by suspicions.

"Thanks," he said, finally. "That would be a help, but, aren't you interested in Balchin's dig?"

"To be honest there's not that much to see now that they've taken the body off to the lab," David replied.

"Okay, but I'll warn you that I'm expecting to find a dead calf or rotting cow." Harry would have liked to see distaste cross David's features so that he could categorize him as a squeamish city dweller, but it did not happen.

"That's okay, my beef is usually dead when I eat it anyway," David quipped. "Where is this ex-cow meant to be anyway?"

"This field here," Harry said pointing. "I saw a trail leading to what looked like a recent dig when I was in the helicopter, this morning."

"You were in a helicopter?"

"Yes," Harry tried to make it sound casual. "Jane Appleby, the reporter, took me up with her friend. I managed to take aerial photographs of the whole farm."

"It sounds excellent," David enthused. "I've never been in a helicopter; you'll have to tell me all about it. I'll just fetch a spade; hang on a minute."

When David returned the two of them talked animatedly about Harry's flight, with some of camaraderie that they had shared in their youth, before paranoia had become Harry's master.

Bent in the easy union of labour, they failed to notice that Jonathan had brought Danny to find them.

"Hello," Jonathan said, stopping the wheelchair next to them and applying the break. "What are you two up to?"

David looked round and straightened. "Harry thinks that someone may have illegally buried a dead cow here," he replied, "and we're just trying to find out."

"It's not a cow," Danny said softly and certainly from his chair. The others looked at him, wonderingly. He had sounded very sure of himself.

"Do you know what it is, Danny?" Jonathan asked.

"No," he replied, "but it's not a cow."

"Let's see then, shall we?" Harry said, turning and bending harder to his task.

The two spades worked in unison, flicking the recently settled earth once more into motion, until Harry's spade ceased its rhythm. It stopped, scraped a bit more, and then was flung aside.

"Oh my God," Harry breathed, "it's another body." He turned around, and was just in time to see Danny standing next to him, before the boy's legs crumpled, and he fell onto the grave.

Sleepers Awake

Danny lay between the crisp white sheets of his bed, fast asleep.

The doctor had awoken Danny once, just to check him over, and everything had seemed to be fine; he was merely sleeping very deeply.

Two hours had passed since the doctor had left and Mrs. Jones had hardly left her son's side. She continued to watch, sitting on the edge of his bed, as a seemingly untroubled sleep calmed his brow.

She reached down and stroked his hand. Immediately Danny's body careered upwards, his clawed hands grasping onto the lapels of her cotton shirt. Instinctively she tried to pull away, but her son's alarming strength would not allow it.

Danny was panting hard, and she could feel his taught muscles trembling. He looked terrified and stared around him, as though searching for something, his eyes lingering on his father's camp bed.

Danny's head slowly turned on her in confrontation. Wide black pupils glared into hers, and they screamed of a desperate void.

Scared for herself, and for her son, Mrs Jones was unable to breathe a word that might break the spell her son was weaving.

As sweet and thick as pear drops, her son's sick breath violated her nostrils as the tremor of his hands shook her frame—tremor building upon tremor until, with a wrench and an explosive gasp he tore himself free from his rigor and fell against her, sobbing.

"Help me Mum," he blurted through his tears. "The stones don't want us there. They never have, but, now, I'm alone and I'm afraid. I can't sleep in peace; the stones won't let me. Help me. Please." He slid down into her lap where the tears and sobbing possessed him completely.

She laid a hand across his head and spoke to him of all that was secure in his life, until she felt his sobs subside and she knew he had fallen asleep, once more.

Having laid her son carefully back in bed, she went to telephone George.

Time To Relax

Harry lowered the phone back onto its rest and returned to the kitchen.

"And what did our Miss Mason want with you this time?" George asked, lowering his evening paper.

"She was asking me to have lunch with her. She thinks we should meet, so that she can tell me exactly what our legal position is."

"Are you going?"

"Yes, I thought I would." Harry scraped back a couple of the kitchen chairs and sat down to bridge the gap with his legs.

"Well done. I'll tell you what—I'll be glad to know where we stand legally with all these dead bodies appearing on our land. Not to mention all the weirdo's who keep trying to break in to look at them."

"Yeah," Harry chuckled, "and people think farming is boring." A black Biro was lying across the crossword in the Cornish Recorder spread upon the table. Harry picked it up and tapped it on the tabletop. "How's Danny Jones doing anyway?" he asked. "I didn't have a chance to ask before."

"His mother still sounded worried when she rang," George said, folding up his paper and tossing it lightly back onto the table. "It sounds like he hasn't done much but sleep since he got back. She said he'd only woken up once, and then he scared the life out of her."

"Why, what happened?" Harry asked, sitting up in his chair to take more notice.

"I'm not sure exactly," George said, shrugging his shoulders, "but she said he was ranting on about the stones and saying that they didn't want him."

"Weird."

"You can say that again," George agreed. "But worse is to come." He grinned and tapped his teeth with his fingernails as he waited for his son to ask the question.

"What?" Harry asked, suspiciously.

"She wants to come here tomorrow to look at that body you dug up today."

"And?"

"And, seeing as you dug it up, I think you should be the one to show it to her. She's going to flip her lid, though, when she sees those marks on its wrists."

"Well why did you tell her she could come round then?" Harry asked in exasperation, getting up to fill the kettle.

"I couldn't really stop her. I tried, but, she said that if her son was allowed to visit the site why wasn't she? Could I argue with that?"

"You could have tried. Anyway, let Balchin The Black deal with it—anything that's dead is his department. Besides I've got other things to do tomorrow."

George skidded his mug across the table to indicate that he would like another cup of tea. "Such as?" he said.

"Such as, seeing Heather Mason and doing the evening's milking, and about a dozen other things." Harry picked up the mug to rinse it.

"Well I hope you're going to be around the day after then." George said, sniffing.

"Why?"

"Because it's our big day, of course. That old stone of ours is due back sometime in the afternoon." He stopped, struck by a sudden thought. "Hey. You don't think they will want to be paid for it do you?"

"I don't know. I suppose they may want their money back." Harry replied, pouring out the tea.

"Great!" George sighed. "Well it had better help us keep the farm." George tried to push aside the thought of losing more money.

"Anyway, besides that," he continued, "that old body is being brought back then, as well. So you'll have to be here. They want to see if it's related to yours."

"Yes, I know," Harry said, bringing the mugs back to set on the table. "Balchin didn't seem to keen about that, did he? What happened about it in the end?"

"Well, as you say, he seemed to think that it was a totally different find, but when Matt pointed out that they both had marks on the wrists and followed the trail you found, back towards the burial site, the others all sided with Matt." George took a sip of his tea, whilst Harry tipped his chair backwards to rest his knees against the table.

George continued: "The long and short of it is that they're going to bring the other body back and see if they could both have fitted in the pit." He paused, before venturing onto delicate ground: "At least there's no talk, this time, of Sarah Nancarrow, or your possible involvement."

"Huh. That's reassuring isn't it?" Harry grunted. "They obviously don't think even I could be so stupid as to kill someone, bury them, move the body, bury it again, and then dig it up once more, in full view of an audience."

"But someone moved it, and moved it recently. Perhaps it was those travellers."

A silence born out of private thoughts going off at tangents to the conversation fell across the table. George was the one to break it: "Do you think Jane would want to cover the story?" he asked.

"What story?" Harry asked, obviously still lost in his own thoughts.

"Well I did think that she might want to know that we've got all the washing done and it's still only Wednesday, but, then I thought, maybe she'd be interested in the story of the stone and the body coming back the day after tomorrow. What do you think?" George used sarcasm rarely, but effectively.

"I don't know, do I? Would you be willing to let her?"

"If you like her, I don't see why I shouldn't."

"Okay," Harry said, "I'll give her a ring tonight or tomorrow."

"If you can fit it in amongst all those other things you have to do, of course," his father grinned.

"Of course," Harry nodded seriously.

George patted the tabletop and got up. "I think I'll go down to the pub in a minute," he said. "Do you want to come?"

"No thanks, Dad," Harry said, still sipping his tea. "I think I'll have an early night and try and get some sleep. I'm still not used to these early mornings yet."

"You should come along," his father persisted. "It would do you good to socialize over a few beers. If you want, just you and I could go somewhere together."

"No thanks, Dad. I wouldn't want to cramp your style with the ladies."

"It doesn't upset you that I flirt a bit, does it? None of it is serious you know, apart from Linda, maybe. I still miss your mother you know: there isn't a day that goes by without me wishing she were still here."

Harry got up, and would have put an arm around his father's shoulders, but, he couldn't quite bring himself to do it. Instead, it turned into a companionable slap on the shoulder, as he slipped past to wash his cup. He tried to lighten the mood. "Don't worry, Dad. I know how much you loved Mum; and, I quite enjoy being known as the son of the local Valentino."

"Oh, come on," George laughed. "I'm not that."

"I'm afraid you are, Dad, but don't worry I won't spread it any further. Besides, I really don't mind. I'm glad you enjoy yourself, but how I would feel if you wanted to re-marry or live with someone else, I don't know. We'll just have to wait and see."

"Well, you're going to have a long wait," George laughed. "Are you sure you don't want to come along? I think I can manage to stop the women falling at my feet for one evening."

"No thanks, Dad. I wouldn't want to upset their day."

"Okay then," George said, "you can't say I didn't try." He picked up his coat and walked towards the door, "I'll see you later then."

Harry went into the lounge and switched on the television. I like my father, he thought.

Opprobrium

Harry waved to Mrs. Jones as her car passed his and entered their yard. Just in time, he thought happily, let his father cope with that one.

He drove along the summer roads and through the tunnel of tree branches that hung over his favourite lane. Somehow, it always made him think of a picture book his mother had read to him as a child. It was of Alice in Wonderland, and the picture showed the White Rabbit running down a leafy burrow, which looked just like this arboreal canopy of green solace.

Such a journey never failed to lift his mood, because it spoke to him of a living past: one in which these trees had breathed, and grown and where Robin Hood, himself, must have seen almost identical images, as he trod his forest paths.

Harry's mood couldn't have been raised much higher on this day, but, none the less, it was eased up a notch or two by his drive, so that, by the time he parked in Penzance, people noticed him; not because of his size or good looks, but because of his huge grin and the happy aura within which he was enveloped.

The café was not hard to find, but Heather Mason was: she wasn't at their reserved table, but, undeterred, and hardly thinking of farm matters, Harry ordered a coffee and sat down to wait.

Ten minutes later a slim lady, of medium height walked into the café, the lines of her light beige suit, hardly moving as she glided in and waved to him. He half lifted his hand in return, feeling self-conscious as she came towards him. She dropped her bag over the back of the carved wooden chair. Something seemed familiar about her, but Harry did not know what it was.

She removed her sunglasses as she sat down, and reached out to touch his hand. "Hello Harry. Remember me, Sarah Nancarrow."

If, indeed, it were a long dead skeleton that stroked his hand, it could not have had a more devastating effect. Harry jumped to his feet and pushed himself from the table, ramming the man sitting behind him, painfully, into the edge of his table, and sending Harry's cup crashing to the ground flinging brown steaming coffee across the grey tiles. Harry stood gaping, "It's not you, it can't be you," he managed.

The waiter and the cashier ran to pull the table away from the trapped man. Who, although smaller than Harry by at least four inches, immediately turned on the Goliath—beside himself with rage. Grabbing hold of Harry's jacket, he whirled the unresisting form around. "Who the hell do you think you are?" he roared.

Harry, sight blurring, staggered from the attack. Flesh on fire and head wrapped in screaming images from the past he could do nothing to defend himself. Grabbing at his head, he tried to steady his thoughts and hide from the world, but knocked his aggressor back with the movement. The man flew and, although the table he hit wasn't designed to be one of the collapsible variety, that's just what it did; sending its contents skimming over the floor and the man sliding to the coffee drenched tiles. The waiter grabbed hold of his slippery customer, trying to prevent him from resuming his attack on Harry, but, he needn't have worried—the man may have blustered, but he did recognize overwhelming strength when it threw him around.

Heather, nee Sarah, took hold of Harry's arm. "It's okay," she told everyone, "He's just had quite a shock. Don't worry he'll be alright." She took his other arm and carefully sat him down, as the waiter righted the table and set everything in order about them.

Harry could do nothing but stare blankly at the ghost sitting opposite.

"I'm sorry it's been such a shock, Harry, but I couldn't think of any other way of doing it."

Harry sat in silence, as the waiter approached them once more.

"Can we have two more coffees please?" she asked, giving the waiter a small, apologetic, smile.

"You see," she said turning back to Harry and placing a handkerchief next to his coffee stained hand, "all those years ago I just needed to get away, and I needed to get away in a manner that would stop people from following me. The best way of doing that was to make people believe that I was dead, and, to that end, I'm afraid, I used you."

Harry's jaw tightened, but he said nothing.

"I suppose I always used people," she continued, "but you were special—you had a bit of a bad boy reputation. I needed that, and I thought that I could use your stone circle to my advantage. I thought that if it became known that I took part in ritual sacrifices, then people might believe that the same thing had happened to me. I even spread gossip about our games myself, just to make sure everyone knew."

The waiter returned with the coffees, and, as the steam wrapped itself into Harry's nostrils, he became more aware of his surroundings. Slowly the turbulent images that were being dredged up from his memory, and recreated by the words of his bette noir, ceased to dance before his eyes. He held up a hand. "Hold it," he said. She stopped and looked at him. He stared back. There was no doubt about it; she was the same girl he had loved and supposedly killed all those years before. He took in the long dark hair and elfin features. Still beautiful, he thought, bitterly.

"Why are you back here now?" he asked.

"Because, even though I thought I wanted to run away from here forever, I still became homesick."

Harry sank his head into his hands: even after all these years, there were still similarities between them.

"My grandparents had died, and so it was safe to come home," she continued. She rooted a cigarette packet out of her bag and offered it to Harry. He looked up. He was loath to take anything from her, and he had stopped smoking years ago, but he could use one right now. Any sort of crutch his raging emotions could lean on would be well received. He took the cigarette and lent towards the proffered light. Familiar scent lifted from the hand that held the lighter and wafted from the nearby hair to shake Harry's hand with conflicting emotions. Sarah steadied his hand with hers and stilled the wavering cigarette in the flame. The touch again stunned Harry's senses, and he sat back as quickly as possible to watch the smoke curl away from the lips of his childhood's infatuation, who remorselessly carried on with her depressing story.

"I had worked in a planning office in London," she said, as though reciting the telephone directory, "and I managed to get a similar job here. I didn't intend to see you again or have anything to do with my old acquaintances, but when I saw your father's farm listed as being one of those through which the new bypass was to go through, I felt I should try and help you out."

"Do you think this is enough of an apology for the hell you have put my life through?" Menace such as was in Harry's low voice is usually only to be heard in the rattle of a tiger's throat, Sarah noted it and pulled back from the table. "Is that why you asked to see me? To say, 'Look at the good turn I'm doing for you, aren't I nice?'" his voice was raised, as his fist clenched, crushing the lit cigarette and stabbing it into the ash tray.

"No it's not like that." Sarah's body language was shouting that she wanted to run away; Harry was pleased to see the fear in her eyes. She sat stiffly in her chair, arms stretched out, pushing against the edge of the table. "I had to see you anyway," she said, controlling her voice with difficulty, "to show you the legal implications of the bid for your field and your current position. But, more than that, I wanted to show you that I am alive, I didn't die due to that stupid ceremony we played out."

The glare that Harry cast over the top of his clenched fist was not lost on Sarah, but she rushed on regardless. "I didn't want to risk the possibility that you might carry on feeling guilty for something that didn't happen, something that was just my own youthful and stupidly vicious creation."

Harry rose slowly from his seat, and lent his long frame over the table towards his persecutor. "I'd love to say that I never felt guilty about the thought that I might have killed you," he hissed into her ear, "but I'm not as good a liar as you are, or were; and I did. I felt guilty throughout my life. But, here's a thought Miss. Mason or Nancarrow, whatever you call yourself. I have a friend who's a reporter, and they might find your version of events very interesting." He pushed himself erect and stormed out of the café.

The adrenalin that had been held in check for so long, rushed around Sarah's sagging body, shaking her wilted frame. She clutched her coffee cup tightly and tried to stabilize herself. She did not hear Harry's return or see him striding up behind her; she merely felt the sudden pressure of him leaning on the back of her chair. Her muscles clenched into instant readiness.

"Why did you call yourself Heather Mason anyway," he demanded under his breath.

"My immature sense of humour, I suppose," she said, carefully and steadily, still staring at her cup. "I ended my old life tethered to a stone. A mason is someone who shapes and breaks stones, and Heather was as close to tether as I could get."

The seconds ticked slowly by.

"Funny girl," he said, pushing himself away. "Very funny." He snatched the forgotten car keys from the table and left her for the last time.

Sarah opened her hands and looked down at the cup; its handle was broken in her hand and a small trail of blood dripped from her thumb.

Nemesis Draws In Her Net

Balchin came back to the field from the farmhouse, his mind deep in thought. What was he going to say about the bodies, to the others? If he persisted that the two figures were unrelated it would be easy for him to be disproved, and his reputation would be damaged. It would also be severely blighted if they found that he had moved the boy's body away from the adult's. Set against that there was the harm that would be done to the Druidic order if it were generally known that this priest had gone to his death sharing his blood with, what they now knew to be, a young boy. Catch twenty-two: either the order suffered or his reputation.

Assuming that he was not prepared to die for his cause, there were only two ways he could see out of his predicament. The first would be to suggest that the learned Druids had been attempting some very early form of transfusion and the unfortunate, but noble, priest had died whilst trying to save the boy's life. The second, although not so favoured option, was that the two had been ostracized by their community for their practices, and had been buried away from their oak groves as a punishment.

He would just have to play it by ear, and if possible try to get the first option accepted. No matter how infeasible it sounded, it saved everyone's reputation, and what the press printed first the public were most likely to remember.

Balchin joined the others who were gathered around the pit and the two grey and ancient bodies lying next to it on the palate. He could not help but shiver when he saw the pose in which the technicians had entwined the two abominations: the exact same formation that he had torn apart and tried to scatter.

"That was the laboratory on the phone," he said. "It would seem that the scratches on the antler are compatible with it having been used as a tool. They've dated it to about, 2,500 B.C."

"That's old," George said.

"We're talking Early Neolithic," Matthew informed him. He rose from squatting beside the pit and turned to Balchin. "The palate is ready to be lowered, and Doctor Robinson says that they're in the right positions."

Balchin looked down on the two frames of deflated flesh, the smaller one enclosed by the adults protective arms. They were not in the right positions as far as he was concerned.

"Well if that's the case let's lower them into the pit, and see if they fit," he said brightly.

Several minutes later and, several miles away, Danny Jones turned over in his bed, a contented smile creeping over his face.

Noticing that he still had specks of her dried blood under his fingernails, his mother bent to caress his hand, but something felt wrong. At first she didn't know what it was, but then she realized that the now familiar tension, which had lain within her son for so many days, had dropped away, leaving his body relaxed and his breathing deep and easy.

Despite the dark vile marks, which like stigmata, still marred her son's wrists, she suddenly felt quite certain that he was going to be all right. She stroked the hair back from his brow, and his eyes half opened. "Two to the power," he smiled.

Matthew was taking lots of photographs, as were the assembled press photographers.

"It seems as if the bodies fit together quite well, Mr. Balchin," Jane observed.

"Yes it does. It certainly looks as though someone may have vandalised this extremely valuable find; one that may well throw some of our theories on ancient medicine into disorder.

"Really? Why do you say that?" Michael asked, from behind Jane's shoulder.

"Because," Balchin said, clasping his hands behind his back, "the marks on the wrists, obviously, signify some sort of bloodletting ceremony." He paused for effect. "We could well be looking at the first, unfortunately unsuccessful, attempt to perform a blood transfusion, between humans."

The short silence was followed by an explosion of voices.

"Wow," Michael said, starting to write furiously.

"Are you sure, Mr. Balchin?" Jane asked.

"No I'm not. It is just a supposition," Balchin, said calmly, "but none the less, a plausible one."

"I'd hardly say that!" Matthew interjected. "Knowing the Druids for the blood thirsty lot they were, I'd be far more likely to think it was a ritual sacrifice."

"Maybe you would," Balchin said, deliberately drawing out his words to slow the conversation and give more weight to his speech. "But, as I said, it is only a possible theory of mine, based on my extensive studies of this period and culture. Studies, I may add, which gave me the experience to lead this investigation."

His barbed comment was noted and Matthew turned back to his camera.

"Do you believe, then, that the druids could have been that advanced, Mr Balchin?" Michael asked.

"I know that although modern science has discovered many wonders it is also rediscovering a natural law which the druids assuredly knew and manipulated."

"Such as?" Michael persisted.

"Look to your herbal remedies—nature's laboratory at work. Look to inoculations—like cures like, the body heals itself."

"What do you think the dating of the antler means, Mr. Balchin?" Jane asked, holding her tape recorder towards him.

"It merely confirms what we already guessed," he replied smiling. "That the circle is much older than these bodies. Like the other circles in the area, it dates from the Neolithic period. We can safely say now, that this circle is indeed an ancient monument, and should, in my opinion, be preserved."

"What do you think of that, Mr Penton?" Jane asked, turning to George.

"I'm obviously very pleased," he replied. "I'm glad that the circle my family has been preserving for so many generations, is the genuine article. I'd also be pleased if its preservation meant that I didn't have to lose my field."

Jane nodded her understanding, and switched off her tape recorder.

Michael tapped her on the shoulder. "Hey, you," he whispered in her ear. "I didn't think this story was worth covering anymore."

"I didn't say that did I?" she said, slipping the recorder back into her pocket. "I said it wasn't worth covering until more was discovered about the body."

"Yes you did, and on the very day you said it a television crew turned up."

"Nothing to do with me. Anyway they only reported what we had."

"And now you're back."

"Of course—this is the grand finale."

"You have an answer to everything, don't you?"

"Yes I do. Anyway," she said, smiling up at him, "what's it got to do with you?"

"What's it got to do with me?" Michael laughed incredulously. "The cheek of the woman. Come over here and say that."

Harry emerged from the house feeling totally annihilated. With dreams filled with sad and desperate images of ghosts, blood and stones, and the scene from the café replaying through his consciousness, it had been impossible to lie in.

Why, just when he had been feeling better, did his past have to catch up with him, flay him down to his fears and expose his shame to the world?

He had always feared that Sarah might have run off and died somewhere from her injuries, but he knew that she had begged for those wounds. Her returning to tell him that she had picked him out from the crowd for his gullibility, made him feel much more wretched. She had known that she could make him love her—make him do anything for her, even kill her if she asked for it; and she had been right. All the time that he had known her, she had him wrapped around her finger and had used him like a puppet, strapped to her hand by his own, unwitting devotion. Well she was going to pay for it. He and Jane would unite and expose the skeleton in his cupboard for what she was, and clear his name in the process.

He looked around for Jane, and saw her standing in the middle of the field with Michael Thornton. He walked towards them and saw Jane laughing as she clutched onto Michael.

"Err, Jane," Harry tried.

Jane turned her head toward him, but maintained her grip on Michael's lapels. "Oh hello Harry" she said laughing at him. "I'm sorry we were in a press conference"

"Well it feels fairly pressing to me," Michael laughed.

"Hey. Watch it!" Jane said, laughing and giving his lapels another vigorous shake.

"Err. It's okay. It wasn't important." Harry turned and wandered back towards the house within an inner darkness. Why did she have to laugh at him? Why did women always laugh at him? They spoke to him and shared their lives with him at their convenience, and then laughed at his impudence when he dared to smile with them. They saw the power they could wield over his emotions and then they threw him away.

He slunk back into the house, a fallen man.

Marian and her entourage arrived at the farm shortly after Jonathan and David.

Marian was not feeling well. There was nothing wrong with her physically; it was just that she felt totally drained and defeated. More-over, she felt as though John, the only man she had ever loved, had been defeated as well. This last piece of work, the one that he had attached such passion to, was being returned, unchanged and untouched, to its home.

Since this stone had been dragged into her world, her entire life had been turned around and torn apart, so that, in the end, she too had been forced to turn around and bring this thing back to where it had started.

She hoped, somehow, that returning it to the start, might also turn her life back, and all the disasters that had occurred to her would never have happened. It was impossible, she knew that, but this stone did have strange powers, which she could not ignore. Almost every time she had touched it, she was somewhere else, someone else: like herself, and yet not.

She stepped out of the cabin of the lorry, to see two men approaching.

"Hello Mrs. Dally. I am Alexander Balchin. I'm glad to see you made it alright." The speaker held out his hand, and Marian shook it tentatively.

"Hello," George said, in turn holding out his hand. "George Penton. I was sorry to hear about your husband. From the little I saw of him, I thought he was a very nice man."

"Yes he was," Marian said, biting back the threat of tears. "Thank you Mr. Penton."

"Call me George, or I won't know who you are talking to," he said grinning.

Marian smiled and nodded. "Okay," she said.

"We'll have to go the long way around, I'm afraid," George said. "The last time we just drove across the field, but now there's this pit in the middle of it and we're trying to preserve the stones in the circle. If we take it around we should be able to get in from the field across the river. We've laid down a bit of a bridge across it which should take the weight."

"Fine," Marian said. "Whatever you think best. You'd better have a chat with Henry, the driver, first though."

Mrs. Stanton and Mr. Dart stepped out of their car as Marian was speaking and came round to join her. "Oh, I hope you don't mind," Marian said, "But I've brought along my mother and a friend of the family, Mr. Dart."

"Not at all," Balchin said, "as you see we have collected quite a few supporters ourselves; including a few members of the press.

Marian nodded and looked about her. A number of the people had gathered around the lorry to look at the stone, but one was hanging back and staring not at the stone, but at her. Marian lightly pushed her way through the onlookers to stand in front of the astonished spectator.

"You," Marian said, softly. "I know you." However, the other didn't reply. As motionless as a statue she merely stood with her hand partly raised, as though expecting a gift.

Carefully, Marian reached out towards the open hand, half expecting it to dissolve at her touch.

The other found her voice: "I know you too."

"I know this sound weird but I seem to know you from my dreams," Marian whispered. "Who are you?"

"Jane Appleby—I'm a reporter." An embarrassed laugh escaped her lips, "And I know this sounds silly, but, when I saw you, I thought you were me," but Marian did not laugh, she nodded.

In union, clutching hands, they tried in silence to gather their thoughts and an explanation.

Jane was the first to speak. "When you had the stone," she said slowly, trying to grab onto the words without forgetting the thought they were trying to describe. "Did you keep it on a tiled floor in a white room?"

"Yes I did." Marian's lips parted in wonder. She took a step back and looked hurriedly about her for the stone. There it was in the field across the stream, a tooth of the earth ripping through its green gums to stab into the blue sky above, the sister to her own stone, which had lain in the studio with the incongruity of a black denture in the white sterility of a dentist's surgery. There it had seemed out of place, but, here the setting was perfect and familiar, very familiar. The import of the familiarity struck home. "Then did you stand against that stone and look up towards the hill and across to the wood?" she asked urgently, hardly daring for the answer her sanity craved.

"Yes I did," Jane replied, in excitement. "I did." She opened her arms and Marian fell into them, each one sobbing on the others shoulder in relief and joy.

The others looked on in astonishment, and Michael was about to intercede, but George lay a restraining hand on his shoulder.

The two women parted, but, still held one another's arms, and searched each other's face.

"There was someone else though wasn't there?" Marian asked, wiping away a tear.

"There were many others, I think," Jane replied, uncertainly. "But, eventually, you were the main one, and I don't think we will find the others I saw in this time."

Marian smiled. "At least if this whole world that we live in is mad, we know we're not."

"Not much, anyway," Jane said, giving her spiritual doppelganger another hug.

With linked arms they turned and walked back towards the others.

Michael thought that he could have been watching two sisters approach him. "Are you alright?" he asked Jane with concern.

"Yes fine," Jane said, relinquishing her link with Marian. "Everything's just coming together, that's all."

Marian's mother dashed up to her daughter and took her by the arm. "Are you alright, dear," she asked, as they walked away.

"I feel a lot better thank you, mother. And I know I'm doing the right thing." It was true—she knew it with the happy certainty of someone who has just realized that they were still in control of their life.

"That's good news," Her mother replied. "So tell me, who is that woman you were talking to? Did you know her?"

Marian smiled and looked over her shoulder towards where Jane stood with Michael. "Oh I knew her. I knew her very well."

"A bit of a reunion then, was it?"

"A bit."

"So are you going to tell me where you know her from, or am I going to have to die from curiosity."

Marian laughed and put her arm around her mother. "I'll tell you, but only when we get home. Okay?"

Okay. I'll live until then. Anyway, listen. Guess what?"

"I don't know, what?"

"Alfred said this place is just like your house: there are underground streams stretching away from it like a spider's web. Except he says, these streams are much deeper."

"Well I never," Marian said, smiling to herself. She turned to see Mr. Dart near the excavation, divining up and down with a twitching stick, to the obvious amusement of Matthew and his teammates.

She climbed back into the lorry.

"Okay," Henry said, starting the engine, "Let's get this thing unloaded. And this time we'll try not to break your legs shall we?"

The lorry lumbered into the field, its throbbing engine carrying it over and through the rolling grass to leave dark trails in its wake. It stopped beside the smaller stone. "Alright," Balchin said. "Let's see if we can get it across the stream."

"Wait a minute, Mr. Balchin," Peter said. "Before it comes across, do you think it would be possible to get a picture of them standing together. Reunited so to speak. Perhaps we could have you standing between the two of them?"

Balchin considered this and then smiled in a way that suggested he was only complying with the request to humour the others. "Okay," he said. "If it will get you your picture." He looked to Henry. "Would it be possible to lower your stone next to this one?" he asked.

"No problem," Henry replied. "As long as Mrs Dally doesn't mind. It's still her stone."

"No. That's okay," Marian said. "You can let it down."

The stone was lifted and then slowly swung over to rest next to its companion.

"Leave its harness on," Balchin said, walking over. "It can go back up again in a minute."

He stood between the two stones and placed the palm of a hand on each one, smiling at the camera, but even as he did so, his lips lost their innervation and slipped into an attitude of expectant vomit.

In the same way that a person can be alerted to the fact that their stomach is capable of independent motion by a dropping lift, Balchin was now painfully aware that his organs no longer seemed rigidly attached to his body. Warm waves were washing through his frame and stretching him, physically and mentally, between his hands. Crucified, it was as if fine strings were running through his arms to knot and pull on his every organ. Slowly and painfully he slipped between the stones to fall face down on the ground.

Echoes Through Time

An explosion flared and faded away into the nothing from which it occurred, but the ripples it spawned persisted, and slowly spread outwards from the root of their birth. Ripples of time, spreading through nothing and carrying nothing until, stretched and stressed, they pulled small particles of matter into being. The particles coalesced and clusters of barren rock appeared, to be carried along on the waves of time.

Bowled along on the crests, the clusters of rock deteriorated, and, as they crumbled, parts of them mixed with the gasses above and the liquids on their surface to produce, on one rock, life.

Pieces of the crumbling planet could fit into man's hand, and with these he hunted, protected himself and made fire to warm himself within his caves. However, when Man stood upon his rock as it washed through space and looked out into the void that was his past and his future, he felt alone and lost. He needed to be able to chart his passage through the heavens, so that he would remember where he had come from and could determine where he was going. He needed to create a map, and he did not have to look far to find the materials with which to build it.

For years men had sweated to hone the stones into shape; sweated in their labour and cried tears of joy at its fulfilment. Each cut they struck had been guided by love and respect—happy in the knowledge that the finished stones would prove their dominance over the elements of the earth and stand as a monument to their ingenuity, a monument, which others might come, and see.

Placed on opposite sides of the river, as part of their ancient observatory, these tokens of appreciation for the earth were revered for their resilience and imbued with the power of man's faith and expectations.

Technological wonders of their age, the stones were touched and used by multitudes of worshippers and scholars, who came to stretch their minds into the stars and search the heavens. And, as the sweat of their creators and the ancient stargazers ran into the stones, so too did the urge to explore. Their bodies died and their ashes fell to the earth, but their water ascended into the heavens, where their once bright eyes had searched, and fell down in tears of rebirth to filter through the stones, stroke memories into and from the stone's crystal cells, and leave their souls behind.

Created by man, loved by man, revered by man, the stones stood isolated, but used by man to push out the frontiers of his mind into the stars, man also extended his quest through the earth and slowly, drop by driven drop, links of water formed between the stones, and, bound and held in communion by the water that flowed through all, those who had the power to meld their spirits with the stone, could touch other minds at other sites and locate the souls from other times.

On the West Penwith Peninsula, an area rich in monuments to the earth, were two stones of immense power. Previously isolated they had bridged the gap between them by tenuous dribbles of water, but, now, a short circuit occurred—Balchin.

Images flickered past his dazed consciousness, like flipbook cartoons, but these images were not just slightly different, they were vastly different. Pictures, smells, tastes, sounds, flashed through his body and pummelled his unwitting, unprepared senses into submission. Cut off from his own environment he travelled through a hundred others. Times, places, people, crashed through his mind. An exchange of sight, sound and sensation that covered the land and the past. If his mind had not craved for the past, he may have experienced nothing. If he had a trained mind, he might have been able to control it, but he did not, and he could not. His mind raced on, desperately trying to hold onto something for more than a second, until, like an oasis, he found a core of meaning, and slowly the images focussed and converged.

Before him was an open green field, and picked out amongst it was a circle of small stones, which seemed to be acting as a confine for the many robed people who stood within. Balchin knew their identity.

A man lay in the centre, clad in more ornate robes than the others and wearing a wreath of ivy upon his sweating brow. Creased in pain it was obvious from the man's face and frantic breathing that he was dying. A fact clearly not lost on the youth who knelt by the man and held his hand—crying over the prostrate form, in an agony of sorrow.

With a cry the man lifted up from his rest, clutching onto the youth's hand in anguish, where, for a moment, they stayed, seemingly held together in a hiatus of despair, until the boy signalled to the others and lay down beside him. They closed in then, and although Balchin wanted to look away, he had no eyes to avert, and so, within the confines of his flinching head, they slashed the wrists of their two victims and bound them together.

Balchin could not see, but he knew why they had done it. They wanted to share death together. Such was the priest's and the boy's love. However, whereas the stones were bonded to each other and the living by water, the Druids wished to be bound by blood and death.

The stones sensed the intrusion of the blood, Balchin could tell, but they were powerless against it. Like the stones themselves, the two Druids were entities bound together in spirit, the most powerful and natural force that existed, and nothing could tear them apart.

Balchin was a loner, and as the images raced through his body, it made him realize that he, a singular entity, was an impotent force. The scene he was witnessing, the past that he yearned for, was ostracizing him. His theories of unsuitable love would have kept him as apart from the society he yearned for, as time itself.

Unable to stand the pain of the reality that was unfolding before him, Balchin tore his mind away, and tried to regain a footing in his own world by focussing on images of the present. The stones, however, would not let him go, and as Balchin struggled, his mind flared outwards and came into contact with imminent death.

A mind was preparing to die, because there was no longer any hope for it in the future, and Balchin was now standing alongside it as a vague, impotent, spectator, but there was hope, Balchin's untethered mind could recognize it because there was no hope left in his own. His mind screamed 'No!' as vehemently as it could, but the mind that lay alongside his own seemed unheeding of the cry and intent upon its fate. It appeared as if he were to be forced to be an intimate witness to yet another death.

Balchin's whole being cried out against the pointlessness of the other's intended act, and railed against the unresponsive mind. With all the intensity he could muster, he pounded against the fortress of despair with which the other had surrounded itself; and slowly, he broke through.

It had been less than a minute since Balchin had fallen to the ground and, as the others rushed to the side of the violently shaking form, the rigours stopped and the body lay still. His hands slipped down and left behind a shadow of moisture that seeped slowly into the stone and into the air.

David turned Balchin over and felt for a pulse in his neck, but found none. He looked up at the others. "He's dead," he pronounced. "It must have been a heart attack." He looked around at the others as though wishing someone would contradict him, but none did. "We'd best call an ambulance." He looked back down at the body, and, as he did so, an unexpected tear slipped from his eye and landed between the spatters of mud on Balchin's shirt, to spread darkly through the white cotton.

Harry leant against the stone wall of the attic staring at the rafter above him. Finally, from somewhere within, he reached a decision, and, pushing himself away, stood on the chair to untie the noose that had been the source of his contemplation. Stepping off the chair he heard the steps of his father hurrying into the kitchen below.

Printed in Great Britain
by Amazon.co.uk, Ltd.,
Marston Gate.